TOO MUCH
FOR
TOO LESS

AHMED

INDIA • SINGAPORE • MALAYSIA

ISBN 979-8-89475-275-4

Contents

Chapter – 1

Spread upon more than two acres of picturesque landscape environment stood a huge tempting spacious beautiful palace called "THE PARADISE" surrounded by variety of ornamental, selected fruits and flowery plants and very specifically well planned and well planted variation of rose plant, alluring every visitor to glance and shower praises upon their existence.

Owner of the palace multi-billionaire, the richest and highly influential personality of the city coming from the royal family of rulers who once ruled the country "Raja- Mahendernath Bahadur" @ Raja Sab well-known for his love for all irrespective of caste, creed, region, religion, status and who is equally loved by one and all in the society. Raja sab was also renowned far and wide for his overgenerous and magnificent parties organizer far and wide no invitee would dare to miss the invite and consequently "THE PARADISE" and its master was partying now with the elite of the society from the city and neighborhood's PARADISE was totally illuminated on the occasion of one of the Raja sab's two children the second child MEENA KUMARI, who completed her medicine and returned from USA after mastering in heart diseases, becoming a perfect cardiologist and cardio-thoracic surgeon too, to fulfill the dreams and aim of her father to upgrade the existing free medical health care institute serving the poor, which Raja sab inculcated in her daughter since her child hood, after his beloved better-half's death due to the unavailability of a perfect cardio-thoracic surgeon within the reach, more than two decades ago. As a result, today's party by Raja sab was to share the utmost happiness of his daughter's achievement and his dream come true.

Glamorous 27 years Meena Kumari @ Meena slim and beautiful wide black eyes around five feet and 6 inches in height was looking gorgeous in her beautiful party-wear with ethnic touch & was busy with guests receiving their best wishes and compliments but from her eyes it was evident that she was bodily present in the party and her mind was somewhere, as if looking forward to receive someone very special. On the other side Raja sab was exchanging pleasantries with his guests for his success, who were complimenting him for his achievement and also enjoying the most delicious and rare cuisine spread upon a huge dining table and guests were enjoying the buffet dinner, to the south corner of the spacious dining hall a separate table for liquor lovers was placed, serving top class foreign liquors and Raja sab's elder child 29 years old smart tall well-built handsome son VISHWANATH BHADUR @ VB who completed his MBA from Australia very recently was chatting with his group of select friends over beer away from the madding crowd the handsome and daring son of Raja sab, commonly addressed as PRINCE in the society, was a bit short temper and unbending individual. And the present topic of the discussion among the young group over beer was the film industry and people related to it.

Among the guests were politicians from both ruling and opposition political parties, reputed personalities from the judicial fraternity, leading doctors of the city, couple of union ministers, high profile industrialists & business-tycoons, state police heads, film celebrities & sports stars, relatives and friends. And also among the guests were two great personalities, who were busy in discussion, seated in a corner enjoying delicacies' with soft drinks, both were from police department one was the new Director General of Police DGP SHARAT SAXSENA (IPS) @ SS, who took formal charge just two days ago having been transferred from north India a well-known figure in the department for his sincerely discharging duty and the most non–corrupted honest and impartial officer, there was a tale behind Sharat Saxsena's transfer to this state as state elections were to be held in near future and Sharat Saxsena was choice of election commission of India, with him was KARIM KHAN-IPS @ KK, the City Police Commissioner CoP, serving the department in office from past 4 years as city's non-controversial police commissioner.

Attending parties was not new to DGP S. Saxsena but this party was something away from usual parties, the silent atmosphere yet guests seen chatting with one and other, laughing and exchanging pleasantries, though drinks were not restricted but the consumers were seen within very perfect limits respecting the surroundings, servers serving the guests politely, though the party had a big crowd yet the atmosphere was very pleasant and silent. Saxsena was very much impressed by the organizers and was taking the detail introduction of the host and his men.

Karim Khan continuing his detailing, said Raja sab lost his wife more than two decades ago and he did not go for a second marriage reason best known to him (Raja sab) only, moreover he is father of two well settled grown up and highly educated children son and daughter, Raja sab has a vast commercial empire, he has a silk mill and a cotton mill named after daughter, he runs a free specialty charitable hospital, in the name of his beloved wife RANI ROOPMATI as RANI INSTITUTE OF MEDICAL SCIENCES (RIMS), for all and now with the help of his daughter he intends to upgrade it as multispecialty hospital. He runs educational institutions both engineering and medical streams, apart from degree & PG professional colleges and all these educational institutes are under the control of a trust, in the name of his son as Vishwanath Bhadur education trust (VBET) Raja sab is just a commerce graduate but he is intelligent and calculative like a highly educated professional almost all the services are either free or on a nominal charges, Interrupting Saxsena questioned how does Raja sab meet the financial requirements of his free services in institutions like RIMS, VBET, CLOTH MILLS STAFF SSALARIES, and other allied expenditures to which CoP with a meaningful smile said Sir I told you earlier that Raja sab is just a commerce graduate but in practical life he is more than a highly qualified person, he has a multistoried commercial complex in heart of the city name DD mall given on rent and it is in the name of his parents, mother DURGA DEVI and father DHANRAJ and the more unique part of this DD mall is RIMS, VBET, CLOTH MILLS and RAJA garden are partners and each partner gets 20 % share in profits and balance 20 % is reserved for taxes repairs and building maintenance. This is how he runs the show and regarding staff salaries he has other properties given on long lease and his FDs the income from these sources is enough for him to meet staff salaries and other domestic requirements. Sir for your information Prince has a 5-star hotel fully equipped named Hotel PRINCE International given on long lease. Prince has his pent house reserved for him in the hotel which he seldom uses it.... DGP was speechless he commented Karim Khan you are absolutely correct that Raja sab though very less qualified but possess knowledge like a highly educated person, I am impressed, Who looks after this vast commercial set up enquired DGP to which Karim Khan replied Sir there is a fleet of employees comprising of administrative management technical and non-technical staff apart from office assistants and all the activities and day to day works are under the strict control and supervision of the decades old acquaintance RAJIV DHAWAN @ RD, it is said Raja sab and Rajiv are child hood friends from the school days and Raja sab used to mingle with all alike so Rajiv being a only son of a school master was very intelligent and Raja sab developed a liking towards him (RD) for his dignified attitude of being self-reliant...as they grew big they did college also together and after college on account of father's death Rajiv discontinued his further studies and was trying for a job and in those days Raja sab also lost his parents and there was family business of cotton mills so he also did not go for higher studies, he insisted upon Rajiv to join him as his CEO after a little persuasion Rajiv accepted subject to condition that he will be like other employees on salary basis and no special favors to be given and today he is the next master of the Raja sabs vast empire since years the one and only trusted man of Raja sab. Moreover Raja sab has two cloth mills on his two children name. MEENA silks and PRINCE Cotton mill, both the industries are situated in the same industrial area but have a distance of around two miles between them and both have independent administration but CEO for both the mills is one and higher rank officers look after both the industries, only the technical staff is directly under shift managers at both the mills and there is one general manager for both the mills who reports to the higher ups of the mills administration and both the mills are situated near to one another just a couple of miles away. MEENA silk mills is in the southern part of the city outskirts and PRINCE cotton mills is on the other side and also a vast farmhouse existing few miles away from mills having a beautiful cottage for a weekend stays and servant quarters equipped with all required facilities and a van with driver stationed there for staff use. Variety of fruits and vegetables are grown in a farmhouse strictly noncommercial; the farm house is in the name of Raja sab as RAJA GARDENS. Moreover, continuing his assertions Karim Khan said there is a fleet of employees comprising of administrative management technical and non-technical staff apart from office assistants and all the activities and day to day works are under the strict control and supervision of the decade's old acquaintance RAJEEV DHAWAN @ RD, DGP was quietly paying attention to CoPs introductions and later enquired how about Rajiv how many children Rajiv have and where does he reside to which Karim Khan said behind PARADISE in half acre of land around 100 yards away from rear entrance of the main building, exists housing staff quarters constructed and equipped with all required facilities. I came to know that there is a mini function hall also for the families of staff for celebrations and get-together and Rajiv Dhawan resides there only in an elegant three bedroom spacious independent house. Rajiv has only one son well-disciplined, ANIL DHAWAN @ AD 30 years old youth, having completed M Tech and he is a mechanical engineer by profession and also did masters in Chemistry but changed the line later as it was not lucrative for him, Anil Dhawan's father wanted his son to be an academician but he being very choosy had plans of setting up an engineering unit and he did so taking job works for main manufacturers borrowing heavy loans but failed miserably as his products did not match the required specifications project was very big he applied for licenses, Raja sab helped him in every way also in obtaining licenses but in the first attempt itself he failed miserably the samples were submitted to a leading tools manufacturing company and their R & D rejected the produce on technical grounds. Now it is almost six months he has closed down all the activities cleared off his debts with the help of his father and now he is totally idle and I came to know recently through his father that he is planning to go abroad Australia on a job visa in the similar line of activity with a future plan to set up an engineering equipment's manufacturing company after returning from abroad, Raja sab was very unhappy, he called him and advised him to acquire technical knowledge and then to take up a related job for experience purpose, then think of setting up a manufacturing unit of his own in this first attempt Raja sab lost nearly one crore,but he did not claim back from Rajiv and that is the reason he is planning to go abroad. DGP with a smile said you have pretty good knowledge of people in PARADISE to which Karim Khan said Sir this is a part of our duty, every night patrol van visits PARADISE twice and there are specific instructions from department to keep a strict vigil on PARADISE with two visits between 12 midnight to 5 am and to take the signature of the security head.

DGP enquired about other members staying with Raja sab in this fort like palace Karim Khan replying said apart from the PARADISE staff staying Staff report for duty from 6 am till Raja sab calls off the day or 7 pm. What are Raja sabs daily schedule enquired DGP replying Karim Khan said he is out of bed early hours and after a morning routine, he comes down to spacious study which is situated in the premises away from main building in a silent northern side, almost a four rooms flat having a spacious hall to accommodate around two hundred visitors at a time and Babulal is always in attendance till Raja sab is in study driver is given days working schedule and Rajiv Dhawan also takes instructions there only, study is almost like office more over Raja sab's weekly schedule is one day silk mills, one day cotton mill, one day RIMS, one day educational institutes, one day charitable trust, two days at farm house on weekends with Rajiv , Babulal and driver and in a separate vehicle licensed security gun men, including driver of the vehicle following the Raja sabs vehicle whenever he is out but on week end days to farm house three vehicles convoy leaves PARADISE on weekends first vehicle armed security, second vehicle Raja sab and Rajiv only, third vehicle two attendants and Babulal with food items. Who is most trusted person of Raja sab none other than Rajiv Dhawan he deals in millions of Raja sabs turn over but till date there was no complaint from Raja sab said Karim Khan further adding he said, I am not sure but I heard from some reliable sources that Raja sab has made his will and distributed his property among children, relatives and to very close needy acquaintance' details of distribution is not known but I am sure Rajiv Dhawan might have some knowledge? Raja sab's lawyer is Supreme court criminal lawyer Mr. MOHAN VERMA. What about Raja sabs son PRINCE? his behavior and dealings with others, his attitude and so on, is he a spoiled rich guy or a decent person Karim Khan said as far as prince is concerned it is said he is never bending very adamant, short temper and lavish character. Some say he is a bit proud also but in a couple of occasions when we came face to face, he was very polite with me. Oh come on this type of attitude is with every rich youth moreover he is from a royal family so that feeling is natural. Commented DGP and asked apart from this you tell me is he womanizer, gambler, drunker, drug addict and lavish money payer. Karim Khan said Oh no...no...in such incidents I have never heard about his involvement.

The party is also coming to an end. Let's bid goodbye to Raja sab and leave. Karim Khan accepting the suggestion said Ok sure sir lets go.

The duo police officials met Raja sab who was having a discussion with the city high courts chief justice, Justice RAMESH GUPTA on how to curtail the sky rocketing prices of the day to day essential commodities as the poor are suffering from this menace. Raja sab was about to express his views at that moment the duo police top brass interrupted, Raja sab taking a pause thanked them for their presence and bid them good-bye and resumed his discussions.

Meanwhile the DGP and CoP both came out and before proceeding to their respective vehicles walking on the pathway and staring at the rose plants DGP said Raja sab seems to be a very disciplined person and also has a very good liking for horticulture specially for roses. They are very beautifully planted...anyway it was a nice party and having learnt about Raja sab I feel he is a very interesting person, so at the end of the day good night Karim Khan, good night sir replied Karim Khan.

Party at Raja sab came to an end at past 2 am and after the guest's departure Raja sab called Rajiv Dhawan and said please tell the staff tomorrow report duty two hours late. Rajiv said OK sir and bidding good night, Raja sab walked away to his room and Rajiv Dhawan came down to his room dog tired. And fell upon the bed. The day was called off at 3 am at PARADISE and the entire campus descended into the cool breezy summer's dark night, bidding good-bye to the festive atmosphere to plunge into darkness.

Chapter - 2

The next morning as usual at sun rise the inmates were on their toes in PARADISE and it was busy with hectic activity. Clock struck 7 am and as usual Raja sab emerged from PARADISE main entrance with his walking stick followed by Babulal in attendance carrying Raja sabs files and today's newspapers. Close to the alleyway stood rose shrub greeting the visitors with fresh yields and Sandeep (driver) was sitting on the stone bench nearby, busy with his flute playing a patriotic solo, unaware of Raja sab's coming, he (Sandeep) was shocked when he saw Raja sab standing beside him and in absolute surprise pleading for pardon, he said sorry master, please forgive me for not noticing your arrival...

Raja sab resuming walk on the alleyway giving a lovely and lively smile raising his walking stick in air pointing at him said "you have improved in your flute playing skills and chances are bright you will become a big musician one day, good keep it up...

Sandeep in reply thanking for the appreciation said Master, my ambition is not to be a musician but to remain your humble servant till my last breath...

Raja sab giving an affectionate stare said you are gone mad, go out and settle yourself acquiring a good position in the society in life get married and become the proud father of well-groomed disciplined children and live happily thereafter.

Sandeep smiling said, so nice of you for your loving intentions towards your servants but for me my existence will be fruitful only when I die serving you my master I am born to serve you...

Raja sab on reaching the study entrance turning towards Sandeep said, enough of your big talks now go and prepare for a long drive and quietly Sandeep walked away to carry on the orders of Raja sab,

After Raja sab settling himself on the chair as usual, Babulal kept the newspapers and the files he was carrying upon the side table kept near the chair and walks out and again enters the study after few minutes with the tea-pot and snacks (comprising of a fresh apple slice and few dry fruit-nuts). And serves the cut apple pieces in a plate and leaves the study and as per the big wall clock in the study, again after fifteen minutes Babulal enters the study and removed the empty plate from the table and then served green tea to Raja sab in a big porcelain mug and walks out and re-enters the study exactly after ten minutes and leaves study collecting the empty utensils without a word, this was Babulals regular routine, he came out of study and Raja sab was busy going through newspapers, While Babulal was on his way to kitchen same moment Sandeep entered the study and after registering his presence waited in silence for Raja sabs instructions. And after a few seconds turning to Sandeep, Raja sab said go talk to Rajiv Dhawan he will give you today's work to do schedule and accordingly select the vehicle for the purpose.

Sandeep with a positive nod left study, silently making no noise, Raja sab loves silent quiet and calm surroundings around him, noises and loud voice chatting and meaningless laughing on silly comments, remarks and jokes he dislikes, so people whoever visits him make no noise.

Thirty minutes after Sandeep's exit from the study, Rajiv Dhawan entered study carrying files in his hand and a couple of check books of various banks and indicating his presence in the study to Raja sab, he waited for Raja sab to respond, after a few seconds pause. Raja sab said Rajiv pull down the chair and was seated nearby.

Rajiv obeying the instructions, yes Raja sab, today we have the following agenda to follow...

11 am- visit to RIMS along with the chair-person of the institute Ms MEENA (30–60 minutes)

12 noon-Interaction with the Head of the Department's (HoD's) of RIMS and appointment of

care-taker chair-person to look after the day to day affairs prior to MEENA taking full fledge charge and to prepare a list of equipment's, changes if any and any suggestions.

1 pm-lunch and meeting with staff and administration department for up gradation of hospital and requirements.

From there at 5 pm Back to PARADISE and after a couple of hours rest around 7 pm to attend the Australian consulate's get together invite.

Raja sab said in return we will drop the lawyer . I wish to have a word with him. Rajiv Dhawan said OK sir then in that case I will advise the advocate to be mentally prepared to receive you. Raja sab gave a go-ahead nod.

Rajiv Dhawan left the study and reached his chambers called for Sandeep driver and on his entry said Sandeep we are leaving PARADISE at 11 am for RIMS and briefed Sandeep today's entire day's program...

In that case a bigger vehicle is required, I will take out Tata-Safari and will be back in ten minutes after fueling sir said Sandeep.

Yes yes see that vehicle gives no trouble as baby-MEENA is also accompanying us to attend a meeting at RIMS at the same moment. 30 years old, tall, well-built sporting a full face trimmed beard, engineer by qualifications, Anil Dhawan son of Rajiv Dhawan entered Rajiv Dhawan's chambers. Sandeep and Anil were good friends of the same age and almost similar physique, Anil never boasted of being highly qualified when compared to Sandeep, who was just 12th standard. Both exchanged pleasantries.

Rajiv turned towards son enquired what is it junior any specific work, Dad I want to talk to you please spare sufficient time for me to discuss and if you are busy right now then no problem, call me when you will be at leisure.

Rajiv calling him closer said, no nothing specific you can talk, go ahead with the purpose of your visit and turning to Sandeep said You carry on and report to me at 10.30 am.

sir can I make a little request to you? asked Sandeep.

Rajiv giving a positive nod said yes go ahead what is it please feel free and talk.

Sandeep said sir my younger brother informed me that mother is not keeping well therefore I need just two days leave, I will go see her, give her money for treatment and will return the next day.

Did you inform Raja sab ? enquired Rajiv.

Sandeep in reply said no sir I did not dare to do so because the party was in progress and same time

I received the call and now baby-MEENAs hectic schedule so I did not dare to inform Raja sab because I did not intend to leave Raja sab at this busy hour.

RD appreciating said anyway no problem, you did a wise thing now whenever you want you can go and if you need any money ask for it and you will get it.

Thank you sir I would like to go tomorrow by 6 am early morning by bus... and if possible, please give me 25 thousand rupees said Sandeep.

OK you proceed as per your plan and in the evening collect the money also, said Rajiv then immediately turning to his son asked will you spare two days taking the wheel till Sandeep returns, replying Anil Dhawan said why not dad at your command, I shall obey your orders as you wish turning to Sandeep Rajiv declared so your problem and my problem is solved now you are at liberty to go as per your plans and if need be inform and extend your stay.

Sandeep Thanking Rajiv said sir, God bless you for your kind consideration and walked out of Rajiv's chambers.

Rajiv turning to son, now tell me the purpose of your visit.

Anil said Dad last night in the party as per your instructions when I was busy keeping an eye upon the bar counter, I met one of the diplomats to India from Germany and during discussions I conveyed him my plans for the manufacturing of the missile heads and he was very much impressed with my project and advised me to call upon him today after 7 pm now dad if you permit me, I will go and meet him...

After a little pause Rajiv said Well son meeting and eating is no issue but if you make any commitments then you will be in trouble so be very careful in your speech and don't be carried away if any individual attempts to show you heaven upon earth remember son lucrative offers are usually disastrous, seldom clicks, so refrain from giving any commitments.

Anil replied dad please be sure I will not displease you; I am just interested in correcting my mistake, as to why I failed in my last attempt so please don't remind me of my past mistake which makes me feel guilty and offended & I shall not displease you.

Son don't be offended but the loss of one crore rupees during your trial last time was a huge loss beyond my imagination and for a person like me it is irreparable loss expressed Rajiv and continuing, my emphasis is please do not give any promises and commitments which you cannot fulfill that's all. Anil stated I promise you dad I will not repeat the mistake but after gaining the knowledge, I shall not keep idle and will proceed with my plans...

Rajiv appreciating Anils response said Oh my son when you have plenty of knowledge and when you master the art of doing the job to the satisfaction of your clients then none will stop you from doing your business. On the contrary I myself will encourage you. Dear son, always remember to strive hard for status and fortune will follow you were ever you go and status is gained through effective productive sustainable hard work..

Anil nodding his head said I do understand dad thanks for your advice now I will take leave.

Rajiv giving a go signal said yeah please leave but don't forget to report duty tomorrow early morning hours. Anil Dhawan left the chamber giving a positive nod. After Anil Dhawan's departure Rajiv Dhawan was deeply immersed in jungle of confusions thinking about his son Anil Dhawan, as he strongly feels his son misses his mother a lot and is confined to himself and follows his own decisions and very specifically after the loss in business Rajiv Dhawan realized that his son is leading an isolated life. And was worried about his son that he is very much within the society but away from the society leading a lonely life. Rajiv never saw his son moving with friends. He could not assess whether his son is Introvert or extrovert. But he was confident that his son needs plenty of money to correct his past mistake, it was Rajiv Dhawan's hidden desire to give his son bags full of money. Rajiv was back from semi-unconsciousness at the knock of Sandeep. And brushing aside his worry for his son he turned towards Sandeep and enquired whether he is ready to go and receiving a positive reply Rajiv came down to Raja sab and said Sir we are ready, shall we start.

And accordingly, at 11 am sharp the convoy of two cars rolled out of PARADISE first vehicle metallic black Scorpio carrying four-armed security personnel's and in second car Sky blue Tata Safari following the security Scorpio Raja sab with baby-MEENA on rear seat behind the driver and next to driver Rajiv Dhawan with the brief case of Raja sab on his lap. Tata Safari was following security personnel's metallic black Scorpio moving at good speed.

The convoy reached RIMS, a warm welcome was accorded to the founder-Raja sab & chairperson MEENA by all the staff of the medical institute led by Chief of RIMS Dr. Ramesh Chander, administrative officer Gautam Jain and others.

After planned meeting and discussion and hearing grievances of the staff the meeting concluded much behind schedule.

The convoy returned to PARADISE as per plan.

At 7 pm again the convoy left for Australian embassies residence but this time it was Raja sab,

Rajiv Dhawan, security personals only and making his presence known in the crowdy party and after exchanging planetaries with the host and his friends. Raja sab came out of ambassador's residence and sitting in the vehicle enquired with. Rajiv, have you taken an advocate's appointment, yes sir replied Rajiv and added advocate is eager to receive you.

And thereafter silence prevailed during the entire journey and after reaching advocates office Raja sab advised Sandeep to follow carrying the brief case and files and calling Rajiv Dhawan close to him, he said Rajiv I have taken a big decision to be added in the will. Rajiv Dhawan enquired what is it master and Raja sab said wait for a while and you will know everything in detail, Raja sab with Rajiv and Sandeep carrying the files and brief case entered advocate MOHAN VERMAs office he welcomed them with great respects. Raja sab and Rajiv Dhawan took their seats and SANDEEP was standing behind Raja sabs chair, Raja sab turning to advocate said please finish the work fast as I am tired and intend to call off the day as soon as possible. with a positive nod MOHAN took out a file and placed it in front of Raja sab who took the file containing a bunch of Non judicial stamp papers and going through specific papers Raja sab endorsed his signatures on the bunch of non-judicial stamp papers it was his will he said it is ok now you come down to PARADISE tomorrow

7 pm and after dinner with us I will inform my children my intentions in your presence and if required we will make necessary changes and take signatures after their approval, I will close the subject. Raja sab after endorsing his signatures on the will papers returned the file to advocate and turning to Rajiv Dhawan he said I have given your son Rs 15 Crores to set up his industry without depending upon anyone. Rajiv and SANDEEP were shocked on this declaration it was pleasant but shocking surprise for Rajiv Dhawan indeed this was a great news, Raja sab left advocates office with his staff, once again reminding advocate to be in time tomorrow with all required papers at Paradise and with his staff Raja sab was back in the car heading back to PARADISE. During journey Raja sab said tomorrow evening after 7 pm I will discuss with my children and conveying my intentions and I am sure they will not oppose it, still if changes are required we will do it agreeing mutually, on the other hand Rajiv was constantly insisting Raja sab to change his will with regards to the mighty allocation and was continuously saying, master I cannot burden your mighty gesture of Rs 15 Crores, it is beyond my imagination and never in dream also I had desire of receiving this huge gift from your end. Master, please cancel it, Raja sab looking at Rajiv Dhawan said with a smile we have advised advocate to join us for dinner

tomorrow 7 pm and to come with necessary required documents, further continuing Raja sab said we will see tomorrow if my children object then I will change but after settling for a small amount of Rupees two crore, Rajiv looking at Sandeep gave a sigh of relief and Raja sab continuing said Rajiv since past few days I am not keeping well and have a feeling that I may not survive for long hence I have taken a decision and distributed my property among my children relatives and i have also taken care of my loyal staff and you are one of the lot. Rajiv wanted to tell something but Raja sab stopped him from interrupting and said Rajiv I know you don't need anything but your son is struggling to establish himself for which financial assistance is must and I know you can't meet his requirement hence keeping in view all this I have given your son Rs 15 Crore to establish himself with ease without depending upon anyone, SANDEEP driving car was stunned after hearing Raja sabs shocking declaration and Rajiv was worried as Raja sabs herculean gift was beyond his imagination and he said master this is a very mighty mountainous deliberation which I can't afford to shoulder, please master change your intentions in tomorrow's meeting with advocate enabling me to rest in peace. Raja sab said let's wait for tomorrow and continuing further he said I knew you will not accept it but you must realize that you being my child hood acquaintance i know about you perfectly well and hence i have taken this decision and now please don't compel me to change my decision I will feel humiliated. Rajiv was tight lipped because he knew Raja sab is a very emotional character, he loves to help any needy person and feels elevated after doing any favor to anyone directly or indirectly or through his VEER BAHADUR CHARITABLE TRUST VBCT, Raja sab keeps helping the needy persons irrespective of caste creed region religion, needy enters VBCT with empty hands but never exits empty hands. Raja sabs RIMS, VBET, VBCT are the source of his happiness, he renders help to needy and relish his activity, Rajiv Dhawan has seen many a times Raja sab while checking the monthly expenditure statement he feels very much satisfied and never questions the accounts head if expenditure exceeds the allocation.

Car was entering PARADISE Raja sab said Rajiv please call of the day and plan for tomorrows CEO selection for twin cloth mills, we will discuss in details tomorrow, reaching PARADISE all of them dispersed and headed towards their respective destinations Babulal came running and taking Raja sabs briefcase from Rajiv followed Raja sab Rajiv was also walking a little behind Raja sab, Rajiv said by the way master our driver Sandeep is leaving for his village for a couple of days as his mother is not well.

Oh please do give him permission and if he needs any financial assistance, please do oblige, advise Raja sab and also advise him, if need be, he can bring his mother here to RIMS, by the way Rajiv have you arranged for an alternative driver during Sandeep's absence.

Rajiv replying in affirmative said Yes sir my son Anil will take the wheel till Sandeep returns.

Raja sab approving the decision said Fine and then all dispersed.. Babulal after keeping Raja sabs briefcase upon the bed room table came out of the room...

Rajiv reached his house his son Anil who was sitting in the balcony talking to someone over mobile seeing his father coming he disconnected the call and stood up, Rajiv requested his son to call Sandeep and after few minutes Anil returned along with Sandeep, Rajiv taking out a bundle of currency notes amounting to Rs twenty-five thousand gave it to SANDEEP and enquired when he is leaving, thanking for the financial help SANDEEP said tomorrow early morning around 4 am I will leave PARADISE as bus terminal is three miles far from here and first bus is at 6 am sharp, Rajiv said don't worry Anil will drop you at bus stop start at 5 am and go peacefully and further added that, it is Raja sabs instructions that if you need more financial assistance please call me and if necessary bring your mother for treatment to RIMS, Sandeep thanking for everything said God bless you all and took leave with Rajiv and came out SANDEEP and Anil were known to each other since long and being of same age group both had cordial relationship. Anil before bidding good night advised SANDEEP to give him a wakeup call 30 minutes before leaving PARADISE, SANDEEP gave a positive nod and both parted.

Chapter - 3

Sharp 4.30 am Anil Dhawan woke up in response to SANDEEPs call and received the call he said at 5 am he will be near PARADISE car parking lot and advised SANDEEP to take out the car and in return he will drive it back. And accordingly, Anil reached the parking lot SANDEEP was reversing JONGA jeep. Both the young hearts came out and taking a break at road side tea stall both had two cups of hot coffee both were busy in discussions topic was Raja sab and his kind gestures and generosity towards his employees his good deeds and all the way SANDEEP was citing instances and praising RAJA sab right from past till date the helping nature of Raja sab appreciating Raja sabs kind heartedness citing many examples from past till present happenings. Discussions never ended but the journey to the bus terminal ended. SANDEEP boarded the bus destined to his village and thanked Anil Dhawan for his lift, Anil with affectionate looks at Sandeep advised him to call him on his return and he will come to receive him. Sandeep with thanks is assured to do so. The bus left the terminal. Anil taking a U turn drove back to PARADISE and was busy talking to someone over mobile and the discussion came to an end after reaching PARADISE around 6.45 am. Rajiv Dhawan was sipping coffee relaxing on the rolling chair kept in balcony. Anil after greeting his father informed him that he has dropped SANDEEP at bus terminal. Rajiv said OK now get ready by 8 am come down to study, Anil parted assuring to be there.

Raja sab as usual reached study at 8.30 am followed by Ramlal carrying briefcase and today's newspapers. Rajiv Dhawan and Anil Dhawan were in attendance replying to their wishes for the day Raja sab advised Rajiv to follow him, Anil settled upon a chair in visitors' gallery going through today's newspaper, tea was served to Anil as a customary practice for every visitor.

In study Raja sab was enquiring with Rajiv Dhawan today's schedule. Rajiv said master you are supposed to visit cloth mills to select CEO for twin mills. From there you have an appointment with RIMS chief doctors along with chairperson of RIMS from there back to PARADISE at 4 pm and at 7 pm you have an in-house meeting with advocates along with your siblings. Raja sab said Rajiv , we will have a meeting of the RIMS managing committee tomorrow at RIMS only call them and inform them of the change in schedule. We have a meeting with advocates at PARADISE and it is only for mills staff we are meeting at site, Rajiv said yes master we are going out only for CEOs selection. Rajiv lets change the program. We will visit textile mills and there we will decide the CEO selection strategy whether to conduct immediately or to postpone it. Rajiv Dhawan said as you wish master. calmness prevailed for some time meanwhile Ramlal came with tea and snacks while Raja sab and Rajiv Dhawan were busy in discussions, he served tea for both and left and re-entered and left collecting the empty utensils. Raja sab said Rajiv you and your son go and have breakfast and I will also have a discussion with MEENA and PRINCE. Accordingly both came out of study and parted Rajiv signaled his son Anil to follow him and both came down to their cottage and over intercom Anil called for breakfast and it was served if few minutes, during breakfast Anil was telling his father his plans of going abroad after SANDEEPs return to which his father just gave a nod in approval for his plan Anil also requested his father to provide an appointment to one of his friend in any department of Raja sabs vast empire, Rajiv enquired about his friend and his qualification experience and residential address Anil gave convincing replies and RD also enquired whether his friend possess driving knowledge to which Anil replying in positive said his friend also holds a valid driving license, Rajiv advised his son to bring his friend tomorrow morning. After breakfast Anil came out and reached parking lot talking to his acquaintance over mobile reaching parking lot ending mobile conversation, he took out latest model air conditioned SKODIA car and after checking brought out the vehicle and parked it in portico and coming out of the car took a seat in portico waiting hall to receive Raja sab. Clock of PARADISE tower was striking 11 am and after 20 minutes Raja sab elegantly dressed was seen coming out with baby MEENA she was carrying Raja sabs brief case Anil leaped forward and taking brief case from baby MEENA quickly reached to car in portico and opened the rear door of the car Raja sab settled himself followed by baby MEENA and same moment Rajiv Dhawan also reached and sat next to driver, SKODA rolled out security's black SCORPIO rolled out a head. Today's work schedule was already briefed to security people and the textile industry chief was also informed. On the way to cloth mills Raja sab enquired about SANDEEP and was informed that SANDEEP left by 6 am bus and Anil dropped him at bus terminal and Rs 25 thousand was given to him. Raja sab expressed his happiness with a smile and said very good, further discussions on today's selection of CEO for twin textile industry was discussed at length and Rajiv Dhawan suggested for selection through secret ballot. Raja sab accepting the suggestion said OK let us decide at the venue further action plan. Covey reached MEENA silk mills in charge while his administrative subordinates were waiting to receive Raja sab. A warm welcome was accorded and Raja sab settling in chair persons chambers advised chief SHANKAR NARAYAN to come with personal service records of PRINCE cotton and MEENA silk mills along with first level executives and added we shall meet before lunch Mr. NARAYAN left replying in positive. security personnel and Anil Dhawan were seated in visitors' chairs kept for visitors In Front of chairperson's chamber. Raja sab Ms MEENA and Rajiv Dhawan were inside the chamber discussing the CEO selection process appointment is necessary or can be postponed to some other date. As advised Mr. NARAYAN entered knocking the door with few files in hand placing the files on the table he said Sir should I call the required committee member to which Raja sab said Mr. SHANKAR NARAYAN new incumbent is supposed to be picked up from the staff and it is a time taking job and due to day long hectic working schedule and commitment to visit VBET, we will conduct the selection process today after dinner you please come down to PARADISE along with the managing committee members and aspirants for the position we will select the CEO through secret voting. Eligible voters are category 1, 2 and 3 level staff members. NARAYAN accepting Raja sabs suggestion said OK sir we will reach PARADISE by 7 pm and soon after dinner we will take up the selection agenda. With this Raja sab along with his accomplice came out of chambers and proceeded towards car and the convoy came out of MEENA silk mills and took return route to PARADISE on the way taking a break at VEER BAHADUR EDUCATIONAL TRUST (VBET) office in the city limits situated in the posh commercial area, the staff at VBET were little confused and divided on issuing of scholarships selection and disbursement to the new applicants as applications were pouring in for the financial assistance, hence Raja sab was called to settle the issue amicably. Raja sab on reaching VBET without wasting any time called CEO Mr MADAN SHETTY and giving a patient hearing to his problem advised him (the CEO of VBET) to happily consider all the applications for financial assistance and based upon merit and to conduct through enquiry by the public relation officer's staff, irrespective of number of applications, he also advised to call for the applicants meet and declare in the meeting that deserving candidate will be eligible for the financial assistance. Further you also declare that the assistance will be provided after going through all the documents' purpose of assistance required for higher studies and other allied conditions and finally the loan will be given to the selected candidate by the authority on merit basis, CEO Mr. MADAN assured to follow the instructions. After solving VBET issue convoy reached PARADISE around 5 pm, on the way to PARADISE Raja sab confirmed with Rajiv whether he has confirmed advocate reaching in time and said a little change might take place to which Rajiv said thank you master, convoy reached Paradise, deboarding from the car Raja sab instructed Rajiv to receive advocate and be seated in dining hall and to inform him, Rajiv replying in positive advised Anil to park the car and call of the day.

Chapter - 4

At 7 pm Advocate MOHAN entered PARADISE and was escorted by staff to Rajiv Dhawan who was sitting in the waiting area to receive visitors. Having sighted the advocate from a distance, he rose from his seat and welcomed him and said I will intimate Raja sab that you have come. And through a staff he sent the message to Raja sab that advocate has landed, errand came back with a reply that Raja sab has advised to be seated in the conference hall of study and he will join them shortly, same moment office assistant informed Rajiv Dhawan that MEENA silk mills Mr. Narayana along with his team has arrived. Rajiv accommodated all of them in the conference hall.

It was 7.30 pm Raja sab entered in followed by Anil Dhawan who was carrying Raja sabs briefcase and few files in hand, keeping the stationery upon the table he left, Raja sab through Rajiv Dhawan advised Anil to call off thes day.

On Raja sabs instruction dinner was served to the guest visitors around twenty-two members enjoyed the delicious dinner comprising a variety of preparations vegetarian and non-vegetarian. While all the visitors were busy in taking their dinner Raja sab and Rajiv Dhawan sitting in a corner were busy in discussions, same moment Anil came and stood near the entrance seeking permission to enter the hall, with a nod Rajiv called him and coming closer he said father I have called off the day and with your permission can I go out for an hour to meet my friend. Rajiv looking at Raja sab said I think we don't have any work with Anil to which Raja sab said yes we don't have any work. Turning to Anil, Rajiv Dhawan said are you taking any official vehicle to which Anil replied in negative he left. Rajiv said OK you can go but please come back soon. Meanwhile visitors were done with dinner and attendants were serving hot and soft drinks to visitors. A giant size round table was in the center of the hall Raja sab advised all of them to be seated advocate MOHAN VERMA was also advised to join them. After a brief opening address by Raja sab wherein he advised the staff and the managing committee to select their permanent CEO through secret voting. All the staff members and the managing committee with folded hands rose from their seats and urged upon Raja sab to appoint CEO as per his choice and collectively refused to elect CEO through voting. Raja sab never expected this demand and turning to PA Rajiv said Now what is this new unexpected development. And with a pause continuing said, what to do now Rajiv in reply bending towards Raja sab he said master you take a decision select three persons from the group and through draw pick any one person, agreeing Raja sab declared this mode of selection to the staff members and once again there was a stiff resistance from the staff and all of them in one voice urged upon Raja sab to appoint CEO of his choice and we all will accept him gladly. Raja sab bending towards Rajiv whispered shall we declare Narayana to which Rajiv nodding his head in affirmative said please do it master. Then Raja sab stood up and said my dear staff members I thank you all for imposing your confidence upon me though it is surprising that I gave you all an opportunity to choose your Head-of-the-Department but still you all insisted that I should do the task, OK in that case I appoint Mr. SHANKAR NARAYAN as your permanent full fledge CEO do you all agree, any objections please feel free to express. All the staff members present in one voice said Master we accept your choice and we all thank you for your just full consideration, you are always right, hall was echoing with claps, meet came to an end, Raja sab was telling his PA and advocate that meet ended very quickly beyond my expectations and further added now let us finish advocates issue at earliest. Advocate who was standing nearby enquired whether Raja sab has any intention of making any changes in the will, to which Raja sab replied let us discuss this issue in presences of my children and said your presence is also must and if any changes we will do it right now, after conveying my intentions to my children but I am sure they will not oppose it still if any changes inevitable we will do it agreeing mutually, taking a second attempt Rajiv said master I cannot burden your mighty gesture of Rs 15 Crores, it is beyond my imagination and never in dream also I had desire of receiving this huge gift from your end. master please cancel it, Raja sab just gave a smile and turned towards staff who left their seats and thanking Raja sab turned to exit same moment it was sudden power failure it was pitch dark Raja sab was heard saying please be seated and power will be restored in a couple of minutes and in the melee someone went past Raja sab hurting him in an annoying tone he said please don't push just stay where you are standing in pitch darkness don't hurt yourself after 4.....5 minutes power was restored and people present in the hall started screaming on seeing Raja sab seated in his chair with his head on the table top lying motionless panicked staff surrounded Raja sab Rajiv called for the PARADISE ambulance staff and ambulance doctor came running with his kit and on examining Raja sab he said he is poisoned and immediately injected an anti-dote and advised for immediate shifting Raja sab to corporate hospital...Rajiv called and informed RIMS and shifted Raja sab in the ambulance and within 25 minutes Raja sab was in RIMS ICU being attended by a team of expert doctors, doctor daughter MEENA of Raja sab was in the ambulance. On arrival Raja sab was taken to ICU and Rajiv along with Advocate and a few other MEENA silk mills staff were waiting in the waiting hall. Rajiv Dhawan informed CoP about the incident and added that he is at RIMS. All the staff was advised to leave and they obeyed.

Commissioner of Police Karim Khan along with detective chief Dilip Kumar, a 32 years old smart highly educated curly haired well-built exercised figure of 6 feet, reached RIMS in a short time. After taking a report from Rajiv Dhawan, Moving a side commissioner called DGP Sharat Saxena and passed on the information and disconnected. After 30 minutes DGP also reached RIMS and same moment RIMS Head-of-the-Department Dr RAMESH CHANDRA came out of ICU and walked straight to DGP group and before anyone could ask him for Raja sabs health he said Raja sab is on life support and chances are 50–50 and further if he survives the attack then chances are bright that he may slip into coma and as a result after successful effort of saving his life we cannot rule out chances of Raja sab might be victim of partial paralysis...and with this he parted saying I will be in ICU.

Chapter - 5

Doctors were busy with their work and police top brass were waiting in the hospital lobby. Situation was tense. Raja sabs son VISWANATH BHADUR @ PRINCE entered the ICU lobby and came down straight to Karim Khan as he was known to him and enquired, Uncle what has happened to my father how is he now and what is his condition. Many questions in one breath Karim Khan said Raja sab is in ICU and is being attended by a fleet of doctors, when they come out, we will know the exact condition more over your sister MEENA ji is also in ICU. After 50 minutes spine chilling waiting Chief doctor RAMESH CHANDRA came down to DGP group and said: Sir we have done our best and we can confidently say that survival chances are bright patient might not slip into coma, if he responds to medication as per our medication then he will be out of danger but chances of partial paralysis are not ruled out yet, so within next 48 hours we have to keep our fingers crossed, hoping for the best to happen. DGP said Doctor can anyone go and see him Doctor Ramesh Chandra sir at this stage disturbing a patient is not advisable. The patient is unconscious and just going inside to see him means inviting infection so please avoid a visit to ICU as it makes no difference. Best is to wait till he gains consciousness.

Doctor Ramesh Chandra left saying that he will be in his chambers available to attend to any emergency. DGP Sharat Saxena, Commissioner Karim Khan, Dilip Kumar were discussing the next course of action plan but could not reach to any conclusions and finally DGP said let us wait for the forensic report then only we will get a lead to proceed further in detail, to which both the officers, present at the spot agreed. Dilip Kumar said sir you both go and take rest I will be here for another few hours and after ascertaining the situation then I will also make a move. DGP and Commissioner both felt relaxed and before leaving DGP and Commissioner advised Dilip Kumar to leave hospital only after self-satisfaction and if any emergency to call them. DGP left and as commissioner was about to exit Raja sabs son PRINCE came down to KK and enquired about his father's health KK stopped and gave a brief account of the happenings and what all Dr Chandra said and advised him to wait there as his sister MEENA ji is in ICU and she can give an accurate account of Raja sabs health, with this Commissioner also left RIMS

Prince called his set of friends and the group occupied the corner of ICU waiting lobby sipping coffee.

Dilip Kumar summoned his assistant JUGAL KISHORE a young smart 30 years tall well-built bushy hair handsome youth, sporting thin one line mustache and neatly dressed up popular among his acquaintance as romantic character reaching RIMS he confronted with Dilip Kumar stating that, In the entire department why only we two sir there are dozens of high and low rank officers equally intelligent and committed who can handle such situations with ease, then why only we two are assigned job at odd hours when others are relaxing in ACs sir. Dilip Kumar responding to the query said good question my dear Kishore but it is not by choice that we are here we are here because our higher ups need 24 X 7 available result-oriented officers in solving VIP issues. You should appreciate that you have been called to do the job. Our department have good dedicated hard-working officers who can achieve the goal but there is only one drawback with them and that is all are family men and as a result they are bound to give time to their families also, tomorrow if you have a family, you will also be helpless so be cooperative, our bosses have called us as they are sure that we are available round the clock and specifically during crisis we are one step ahead and also, we are not helpless. Kishore prior to passing any comment.

Dr Meena came out of ICU and came down to Dilip Kumar and said Thanks god sir, you have come. I was desperately waiting for you to come and take up the investigation. Dilip welcomed her with a smile and said Madam taking up the case is not in my hand; it is the choice of my superiors. I will exert pressure upon DGP sir to give Daddy's file to you she said and I will strongly protest if the case is given to any other officer or to any other investigative agency declared Meena.

Please refrain from suggesting any names to DGP sir, just wait and see. Now tell me how is your father's condition, Dilip Kumar also briefed her what all Dr Ramesh Chandra said. Yes, the deadline is justified but I have a strong feeling that daddy will come out safely, said MEENA. DK introduced Jugal Kishore to MEENA and he enquired Madam hope Paradise CCTV system is in order. Meena said of course, yes Sir CCTV cameras are in perfect order. Dilip Kumar enquired Madam, have you taken your dinner. In reply Meena said dinner is ok sir but I have a strong urge for a cup of hot coffee. DK turning towards Kishore said, please do the needful. Reluctantly Kishore left the lobby and nearly after 25 minutes came back with hot brew in use and throw glasses. Dilip Kumar and Meena were busy in talks Kishore was aware that Meena was junior to Dilip kumar in college days moreover Dilip Kumar was a well known figure in Raja sabs family as he was from a rich landlord family and his parents and grandparents were good family friends with Raja sabs family, though Dilip was introduced to Meena during family meetings and get to gathers and his introduction was reenforced more after joining college, when she came to know that Dilip is also from the college doing post-graduation final year. People close to Meena and Dilip kumar could note distinctly that Meena has developed liking for Dilip in her soft corner, and never revealed it she was a silent spectator but none could confidently say that Dilip is also fond of Meena. Kishore kept the coffee cups on the table and all the three were sipping coffee. One cup was passed over to Prince who was sitting alone in the corner, as his all acquaintances were gone. Dilip Kumar was advising Meena to share...every minute information it will help us in investigation perfectly and Meena in turn said OK sir I will definitely share if anything crop up.

It was 10:30 pm.Dilip advised Kishore to leave and take rest as tomorrow right from dusk till dawn will be hectic and also advised him to be in office by 8 am and wait for his instructions. Kishore left RIMS.

Dilip Kumar also advised Meena to call of the day and he will take her place in the ICU. Reluctantly she left with her brother Prince who was relaxing alone on the sofa. His all friends were gone. After disposing off DGP, commissioner, Kishore, baby Meena and her brother Prince, Dilip Kumar came down to Dr. Ramesh Chandra's chamber and knocked the door after a few seconds doctor opened the door and seeing Dilip enquired hope everything is fine sir. Dilip responded positively and said Yeah all is well, I have come to talk to you, now there is no attendant at Raja Sab as Dr Meena and her brother Prince both have gone home on my advice. I wish to see Raja sab once in your presence if you don't mind doctor. Dr Chandra Oh why not definitely sir please come with me. Doctor and RK both entered the ICU. Raja sab was on the bed in hospital dress on life support. Dilip seeing Raja sab enquired doctor life support is necessary or just a precautionary step Doctor said sir when he was brought to hospital it was very much necessary but now after nearly five hours there is a positive response from the patient that means he is responding to the treatment parameters are functioning well and I strongly feel that life support system is not necessary but as few other doctors are also involved in the treatment process, I cannot take any independent decision. That means in your view life support is not necessary asked Dilip Kumar to which Dr Chandra replied in positive. After few minutes Dr Chandra left the ICU stating that there is one emergency to attend and he will be in his chambers. On enquiring about emergency Dr Chandra said a poor child patient suffering from multiple cardiac issues admitted in RIMS is supposed to be attended by Dr Bernard Luther world famous cardiac surgeon who has treated many child patients successfully suffering from cardiac problems and he is here honoring one of his friends request, who is also known to me and on my request he requested Dr Bernard to oblige, and as a result Dr Bernard assured to take a look at child patient Anushka therefore we are all busy expecting a fruitful visit of Dr Bernard, with this Dr Chandra left ICU leaving Dilip Kumar alone, ICU staff comprising of two doctors male and female, two nurses male and female and one attendant total five all were seated in their allotted doorless cabin. Dilip Kumar pulled a chair and sat beside Raja sabs bed, going down the memory lane and keenly recollecting the happenings later he came out of ICU and went around all the floors inspected all the exit and entrance CCTV surveillance approach entrance from the main road and main entrance into the hospital, canteen and its staff and during his going around the building he saw security personnel change over in main hall and there was one security guard in the control room seated with his head down on the table...there was only one entrance and exit to the main hall. Dilip observed all this features keenly for self-satisfaction that the assailant has no chance to enter and exit RIMS unnoticed.

Same moment Dr Chandra also came down to the main hall near the 24 X 7 reception and stood there after seeing Dilip Kumar also coming towards reception. Dilip Kumar enquired so your appointment with Dr Bernard is confirmed, to which Dr Chandra said no Dilip, Dr Bernard is going to take up the surgery of the patient for whom he has come then he will take our patient's case. Surgery is expected tomorrow and they are searching for a top-class OT equipped with the latest technology instruments. Dilip Kumar said in that case why don't you invite Dr Bernard to consider RIMS for the purpose. Dr Chandra said i have already suggested to which they said morning 10 am they will visit RIMS and confirm only after inspecting OT. Later Dilip enquired the doctor this change over time is midnight why? Dr. Chandra replying said Sir during morning hours hospital will be very crowdy and peaceful change over is not possible as there will be few minutes pause to the surveillance and security shift is of 24 hours with change over at midnight, Oh seems to be too hectic Dr Chandra laughed and said nothing like that nights at RIMS are usually quiet and calm seldom emergency arising and more over security staff take an unscheduled nap in turns, one after another. Further security, hospital administration and canteen are under the administrative department headed by Mr Gautam Jain. He is MBA and a good friend of Raja sabs PA Rajiv Dhawan. Dilip said somehow security staff shift changeover timings are little confusing to me, in reply Dr. Chandra said as the day timings are usually busy hence, we have decided to start shift from 12 midnight to twenty-four hours shift giving one hour break which the on-duty staff will take with mutual understanding without missing the security of the institution. More over the changeover takes place in the waiting hall in front of the main entrance. Enquiry did not end here DK went on enquiring about maintenance and security arrangement at every floor, CCTV cameras, any other exit and entrance, canteen staffs exit entrance and bringing of canteen food items transport facility at hospital. Waiting place for patients' attendants if more than one attendant visits. Visitors' timings and how many visitors are allowed to visit a patient at a time. Replying to all the queries Dr. Chandra said security and canteen in charge is Mr. Gautam Jain he was appointed by Mr. Rajiv Dhawan PA to Raja sab. Continuing further he said the canteen has separate exit and entrance. They are strictly not allowed to use the main entrance as their day starts at 2 am with staff reporting duty and other kitchen items arriving. And till date we have not received any sort of complaint against canteen administration and staff canteen is hygienically well maintained and preparations are also equally good. The entire hospital staff, patients' attendants and visitors relish our canteen food…Raja sab pays surprise visit to canteen occasionally but Mr. Rajiv visits every month without fail. Gathering a lot of information Dilip commented RIMS seems to be a disciplined health institution and with a smile said excellent administration I am sure no one can enter or exit without being noticed by the security. Dr said Yes very true and thanked Dilip Kumar for the compliment with a wide smile.

Dr Chandra left stating that he will be in his chamber, Dilip came down and settled upon a sofa at ICU lobby watching security change over. At 12.30 am Dilip Kumar knocked Dr Chandra's cabin door and entered in, Dr Chandra was talking to someone on landline seeing Dilip he disconnected the call and replacing the receiver on the cradle welcoming Dilip he asked if everything is ok sir. Dilip with a smile gave a thump up sign said Well doctor I am leaving if anything important please remember I am just one call away from you and by the way when you will be receiving a forensic report of Raja sabs blood sample Dr Chandra said morning before noon. Dilip said my assistant will come and collect the copy of the report after lunch, welcome sir, said Dr Chandra.

Dilip Kumar came out of Dr Chandra's cabin.

And before moving out decided to peep into ICU and he entered and at first glance he saw night duty staff heads down on the tables were in deep slumber, almost all the night duty staff was relaxing except receptionist who was staring at Dilip Kumar in agony as his night sleep was disturbed because of Dilip Kumar and he was awake eagerly waiting for Dilip Kumar's departure his eyes were following Dilip when he was entering ICU, unaware of receptionist's agony because of his presence.

After 30 minutes receptionist gave a sigh of relief when he saw Dilip Kumar coming out of ICU and looking at ongoing security change over and duty allotments, probably security changeover was in final stage, he saw out going in charge taking signatures of taking charge security chief Dilip also inspected canteen he saw 2 staff members sitting in the canteen on enquiry they said they are waiting for the transport van bringing food items vegetables and other allied items for canteen on Dilip enquiring when the van is expected to which the labors replied any moment Dilip just nodded his head and came out of canteen. He came down to reception and enquired with the receptionist whether they maintain the records of people visiting RIMS to which receptionist replied that records of patients visiting doctors for consultation are maintained and other visitors making any enquiry and leaving such visits are not maintained. DK advised him to give a list of people on night duty, to which receptionist asked for 30 minutes Dilip agreeing said you prepare the list and I will once again go around and come back to you, he came down to ICU staff heads down on tables in deep slumber looking at the staff he smiled and after five minutes emerged out of ICU, he entered control room the only security guard sitting was not on the seat room was empty he checked CCTV cameras and after five minutes came out of control room and came down to reception and the receptionist handed over the list of night duty staff, he checked the time it was 1 am Bidding goodbye to receptionist Dilip Kumar proceeded to main entrance, security changeover was almost done and staff was taking their positions, Dilip Kumar was out of RIMS proceeding towards his car.

It was around 2 am Dilip Kumar driving his Scorpio reached back dream house. Around 3 am DK relaxing on the rolling chair sipping water switching off all the lights in a cool blue night lamp atmosphere, going down the memory lane right from the start recollected every move, he suspected the hand of an insider who might have helped the assassin to sneak inside the Paradise. Giving rest to his grey matter he took a short nap of a couple of hours.

Chapter - 6

At 8 am sharp Kishore was on breakfast table cook served a couple of brown bread egg sandwich and a glass of fresh fruit juice, Kishore joined Dilip Kumar on breakfast table after conveying morning wishes he asked Sir what is today's schedule for me, Kishore visit RIMS meet Dr Chandra copy of the forensic report of Raja sabs blood sample, enquire Raja sabs health condition and from there take a police vehicle and along with one male and one female constable visit paradise and collect every detail of guests. why two constables' boss he questioned, for your safety my dear replied Dilip Kumar. Kishore accepting with a nod said that means you are suspecting some insider, naturally was Dilip Kumar's reply, ok now let's make a move. One more piece of advice, please don't drive the vehicle, let the department driver do the job. Both the officers came out of Dream house and on reaching headquarters, before parting Dilip Kumar said to Kishore you better use a police vehicle today for every assignment, as advised along with constables and you will take the constables wherever you go till you come back to headquarters, Now vanish.

RIMS was busy with police vehicles and top brass visiting the institution when they were informed by Dr. Chandra that Raja sab is missing from RIMS. DGP, Commissioner of police, area police and special teams and other allied departments officials made a beeline to RIMS. On information from commissioner Dilip Kumar and Kishore also reached RIMS, seeing the tense atmosphere Dilip advised Kishore to carry on with his schedule assignments accordingly Kishore parted. Dilip Kumar after reaching RIMS was just gathering information. Later DGP, Commissioner, Dilip Kumar and PA to Raja sab Rajiv Dhawan all were seated in the waiting hall discussing the deadline given by the doctors and before the expiry of the deadline patient had gone missing. Dr Chandra who was sweating because of the tense situation was speechless and unable to digest Raja sab, is missing from RIMS. DGP along with his team was on the spot discussing every possibility of kidnapping or murder and also added that as there is no CCTV footage showing Raja sab being taken away or any stranger entering the institution and leaving with Raja sab or Raja sab walking away on his own from RIMS, none of the persons present at RIMS could guess what has happened.

DGP was telling police commissioner Karim Khan how can anyone disappear with a heavily built patient unnoticed in the presence of so many people available around.

Dilip said as per CCTV footage no entry and no exit and Raja sab is not on the bed. With this we can draw only one conclusion, that Raja sab has been kidnapped but not taken out of the hospital the kidnapper has hidden him somewhere in hospital itself and this is possible only with the help of some unknown insider who is perfectly aware of the topography of the institution on how to vanish unnoticed. This doubt expressed by Dilip Kumar gained momentum among one and all present at the scene, as a result DGP took Dr Chandra to task and all the police present at RIMS along with RIMS security were busy searching Raja sab in the hospital, institutions every nook and corner was combed out thoroughly again and again, Dilip Kumar standing in one corner was speaking to someone over mobile and after concluding the call came down to DGP and CoP sitting in the lobby. Dr Chamdra said, around 2. 30 am chief of ICU in charge knocking my door entered inside and panting said Raja sab is not on the bed immediately I came down to ICU Raja sab was not on the bed, we checked everywhere he was not available, I enquired with ICU staff and they were clueless with the help of security staff checked the CCTV cameras but we did not see anyone entering and leaving RIMS. our security personnel also enquired with canteen staff there also nothing abnormal detected. Lastly, we informed CoP sir as he was taking a daily report on Raja sab. Dilip Kumar asked about first shift staff duty hours, was Raja sab present during their duty hours. In reply Dr. Chandra said yes Raja sab was available at that time I checked with the outgoing staff. That means Raja sab vanished in between the changeover period. The DGP said I would like to talk to your ICU staff, night security staff, gate security staff and off duty staff also required along with canteen staff present on duty from 1 am, to be present in the conference hall, to which Dr Chandra agreed and left. Looking at Dilip Kumar he said what is your opinion on this disappearance of Raja sab, has he been kidnapped or left on his own Dilip said it is Dr. Chandra who can give us the exact picture. CoP interrupting enquired are you suspecting Dr Chandra, officer...to which Dilip Kumar shrugged his shoulders and said everything is possible in this world of God upon earth. Don't be philosophical, Dilip comes to the point. The point is sir let us have coffee with Dr. Chandra and I am sure during discussions we will get some clues. DGP agreed and all 4 DGP, CoP, Dilip Kumar and PA Rajiv came down to Dr. Chandra who was giving instructions to his PA to arrange a staff meeting at the conference hall and no one should be absent. Welcoming police officers with a smile he disposed of PA and said in a few minutes staff will assemble at the conference hall. OK then we will wait over coffee, Dr. Chandra agreeing with a smile placed an order for coffee over the intercom. In a few minutes time coffee was served and over coffee

Doctor Chandra was again and again expressing his fear on how to face the media when they will come to know about Raja sabs disappearance. The Commissioner of Police said yes you are right but you have to face the media it is inevitable nodding his head Dr Chandra requested for guidance on how to face the media. DGP said when time comes Dilip Kumar will guide you and turning to Dilip said officer please do the needful, when required. Doctors PA knocking the door entered the chamber and informed staff had assembled in the conference hall. All of them vacated their seats and came down to the conference hall.

Around forty-five staff members of RIMS were present in the hall, without wasting time DGP asked security staff hope everyone is present to which security in charge replied sir except one guard all are present and before DGP could question him reason for his absence security in charge said one person is required to be present in control room. DGP shaking his head said ok. Initiating the query DGP asked security in charge yesterday night who was in the control room one of the night duty staff stood up and said it was his duty he asked him did you leave control room even for a minute replying in negative as per regular practice i gave my attendance when calling off the duty just for five minutes after that I was back upon the seat and this five minute my eyes were on the big monitor which is connected to all the cameras around the building. CoP asked the in charge in these five to eight minutes time if anyone could sneak in and go out without being noticed and said absolutely no chance sir.

The DGP staring at him said when you say so confidently that no one can sneak in and go out, then how come a patient lying unconscious in ICU has been kidnapped and vanished in thin air? In charge said how this has happened we all security personnel are confused. After a few more questions like whether anyone is providing support to the culprit DGP disposed of the security staff with a stern warning that if anyone found guilty will be severely punished. Security staff was disposed next was ICU staff DGP after taking them to task said you people are answerable and i am compelled to take you all in custody for extracting truth and if you people don't want to be subjected to mental torture then voluntarily please confess anyone has extended support to the unknown culprit knowingly or unknowingly, All the ICU staff started pleading that they are innocent, they all admitted that their only mistake is that they took a nap resulting in a big incident, they looked at Dr Chandra signaling him to support their statement. DGP said after through examining the ICU unit and very specifically the bed of Raja sab any lame man can say something has happened well planned and very conveniently with ease executed with the help of some insider, either the patient was kidnapped or walked away without making any noise or someone from inside has extended support to carry on kidnapping. Dilip was patiently attentive following DGPs interaction with the RIMS staff observing staff's reaction. At one point when ambulance driver Mastan Ali was fumbling while answering queries, Dilip Kumar made a note of it but did not disclose his intentions to anyone. Staff's statements session came to an end and again all of them DGP, CoP, Dilip Kumar, Rajiv Dhawan, came down to Dr Chandra's chamber, Dilip before entering the doctors chambers. Dilip Kumar went a little away from the group, made a call and joined the group...

Chapter - 7

Dr Chandra's PA entered doctors chamber and informed the arrival of media and said journalists are seeking your audience sir, doctor looked at DGP Sharat Saxena looking at commissioner enquired who the hell has prompted news to media commissioner replying in negative said someone from RIMS might have done this. Dr Chandra looking helplessly at DGP said Sir now the time has come to guide me how to face the media please, I am totally exhausted. DGP turning to CoP Karim Khan said please help him out in turn CoP requested Dilip Kumar to do the needful. And as advised Dilip Kumar said as the crime took place at hospital Dr R Chandra will open with briefing media and later at one point Rajiv Dhawan will take over and he advised Dr Chandra to talk on health, attack, survival chances of Raja sab and where about of Raja sab pass on the mike to Rajiv Dhawan rest he will handle the situation and turning to Rajiv, Dilip Kumar said you just inform media that his life is not in danger if the kidnapper wanted to kill him he would have attacked Raja sab in hospital itself but he has taken a great risk and walked away with unconscious Raja sab with an intention to achieve something and I am sure he will surface safely sooner or later and for rest of the queries say police has advised not to make any wild statements to media so please excuse us and then call of the media meet, both Dr Chandra and Rajiv were satisfied and came down to press meet.

Media was accommodated in lobby and Dr Chandra after introducing himself addressing media said that security personnel noticed Raja sab was not on the bed and they enquired with night duty ICU staff, who hurriedly came to me and informed me the happening and in turn I informed the police but before concluding let me inform media that deadly attack on Raja sab was very mild it was just,.001 percent and the severity was very minute we doctors team curtailed the spread of poison at its entry point only, In reply to medias question to elaborate Dr Chandra said the murderer was highly knowledge person but over confident too and he thought that simple touch of the substance to the open wound in body will carry the poison throughout the body rapidly, affecting the nervous system, but he was not aware that if the victim is mobile then the chances of poison spreading in the body is certain and here in case of Raja sab this didn't happen. Media requested for a reason for the poison not spreading in the body Dr Chandra said the personnel doctor of Raja sab who was with Raja sab at the time of attack, immediately administered anti dote on seeing the open wound as precautionary measure and rushed him to hospital. Continuing he said you must be aware that any person who collapses due to attack of any ailment and if that patient is provided medical aid within one hour of the attack chances of patient's survival is bright, that is the reason medical fraternity call it as GOLDEN HOUR and this golden hour and precautionary measure saved the life of Raja sab who was brought to hospital in twenty minutes. Now coming to the point, did Raja sab leave the hospital on his own or was he kidnapped and his whereabouts PA to Raja sab will give you details... PA Rajiv taking over from Dr Chandra addressing the media said Dr Chandra has very clearly stated that Raja sab whether left premises on his own or was he kidnapped it is not known. Media Interrupting questioned hospital has CCTV surveillance so with the help of CCTV footage culprit can be identified and apprehended. Replying to the question PA said this particular query please ask the police as we are not aware about the CCTV footage and we are not supposed to comment on this issue as the footage has been taken away by police but one thing is for sure I can say Raja sab is alive. Media urged upon PA to justify his statement PA in reply said if the kidnapper wanted to kill Raja sab then he would have done it at hospital itself secondly if Raja sab has gone on his own then sooner or later he will contact any trustworthy bureaucrat or aristocrat before surfacing in the public. And with this gentleman we called off the press meet.

At the waiting hall Dilip Kumar was prompting the DGP and Commissioner that Dr. Chandra is hiding something important and if you exert little pressure he will spell the beans. DGP nodded his head in acceptance.

After disposing off the media Dr Chandra was again called by DGP and he said Doctor I am not satisfied with your statement I strongly feel that you are hiding some information, In reply doctor said Sir you are correct and he requested DGP, CoP, Dilip Kumar and Rajiv Dhawan to come down to his cabin all the four followed Dr Chandra and settled themselves looking at them Dr Chandra said let me tell you, the wound inflicted upon Raja sab was not very deep it was like a scratch but as the poison was very strong the simple scratch resulted in Raja sabs lengthy unconsciousness after a thorough checkup, we team of doctors arrived at a conclusion that Raja sab is definitely out of danger and might regain consciousness any time before 12 hours positively and we decided not to make public the findings till Raja sab is literally awake. Police personnel raised their eyebrows to register their protest stating indirectly that by hiding facts Dr Chandra has done a great mistake, Dr Chandra realizing their protest said Sir we were sure that nothing will happen to Raja sab but we were scared to declare the findings because Raja sab being a VVIP we decided to wait for some time more and things will be perfect automatically as per our expectations.

DGP said it is OK but remember doctors in such sensitive cases you should share facts with police for a foolproof security arrangement hereafter. Doctor gave a positive nod in acceptance. DGP advised Dr Chandra to continue his statement, accordingly doctor continuing said, around 2 am chief of ICU in charge knocking my door entered inside and panting for breath said Raja sab is not on the bed immediately I came down to ICU Raja sab was not on the bed, we checked everywhere he was not available, I enquired with ICU staff and they were clueless with the help of security staff checked the CCTV cameras but we did not see anyone entering and leaving RIMS. And the last man to leave RIMS was Dilip Kumar, our security personnel also enquired with canteen staff there also nothing abnormal detected. Lastly, we informed CoP sir as he was monitoring the developments related to Raja sab. Rest you all are aware.

Dilip Kumar said Raja sab was very much present during first shift security duty hours. and Dr. Chandra confirmed Raja sab's presence at that time stating that, I checked with the outgoing staff, and they said Raja sab was present at that time. Hence it is clear that, Raja sab vanished in between the changeover period. DGP enquired with the commissioner his opinion on Raja sab's disappearance, whether he has been kidnapped or left on his own, in spite of so many eyes watching surveillance cameras, security staff, receptionist and canteen staff, still we are clueless on his disappearance.

<h1 style="text-align:center">Chapter - 8</h1>

DGP worried over fast developments and yet no clue in hand, he said now how to face a volley of questions from home department executives, it is truly painful. To which commissioner of Police Karim Khan said with your permission I wish to suggest that whatever Dilip Kumar has incited Dr Chandra and PA Rajiv and all that will be carried in tomorrow's newspapers and TV channels so what I feel sir let us stick to same statement so to which DGP gave a positive nod. And vacating his seat he said I am proceeding to headquarters and advised the Commissioner to Reach headquarters after completing his work at RIMS and he left. All the way to headquarters DGP was deeply immersed in thoughts and murmuring why anyone wants to eliminate Raja sab and murmured loudly and why anyone will kidnap him and that too under high security, who is responsible for all this...reaching headquarters. DGP was busy with his routine work. Around lunch time commissioner, Dilip Kumar reached headquarters and after settling in their respective chambers confirmed DGPs availability and seeking audience came down to DGP. Looking at both DGP said it is really confusing, Karim Khan you know these so-called bosses sitting in an AC room are of impression that we are just loitering on the field and it is by sheer luck that we solve the mysteries, any way how to face them is a big question, CoP looking at Dilip Kumar said Sir Dilip will give you a simple idea and you have add spices to it while narrating to home secretary. DGP said please go-ahead and accordingly, Dilip Kumar briefed DGP what all he advised to Dr. Chandra and PA Rajiv and added that the department has still 48 hours in hand and we will touch the bottom. DGP shook his head and said OK now I am leaving to call upon home secretary and after briefing him from there I will call off the day and will go back home pick up my family and rush to airport as my daughter with children are coming from New Zealand to receive them as she is coming alone with two small children, her husband's leave has not been sanctioned but he will be coming after a fortnight. So, gentlemen hope you both understood and if any emergency I am just a call away from you all.

Accordingly DGP reached home secretary's office and was immediately called in taking his seat after exchanging greetings, home secretary Mr Mittal staring at DGP said I am sure you are here to give me some unpleasant news for your information I am facing severe criticism because of your failures, you people are aware that the victim is from a royal family his ancestors were rulers once upon a time and the time has changed but his position and status remains almost the same he is accorded VVIP position and you people are sitting upon files as if nothing serious and important, bosses are anxious to know the minute to minute development and handling these aristocrats and bureaucrats is not an easy task to handle them and at the same time I can understand your pain in solving the mystery but my dear friends my sincere advice to you is act fast leaving no stone unturned and put in all your efforts to solve the mystery within hours not taking days and weeks. DGP sarcastically replied to secretary Sir please take it as granted we will do our best to solve the case As Soon As Possible but during the course of investigation certain barriers have to be handled with utmost care because a minute error might result in delay. Department must cooperate with the investigators. Mittal admitting the DGPs statement said your half of the work is done by the presence of the CCTV cameras and a thorough and keen observation will definitely give you a lead. So my friends please go ahead with a positive mind and your next visit to me must be result oriented listening very keenly. Mr. Mittals critics DGP said sir you are right we are just relaxing doing nothing anyways if I tell you the latest development you will jump out of your seat. Mittal was staring at DGP with eyes wide open as if telling DGP "now what" DGP said Sir last night after Dr. Chandras last round checking Raja sab was on the bed on life support equipment and our chief inspector Dilip Kumar was also there, security staff change over was in process Prince, Meena and PA Rajiv and inspector Jugal Kishore all left RIMS one after another followed by Dilip Kumar after a couple of hours. And around 2 pm ICU duty doctor noticed Raja sab was not on the bed he immediately informed Dr. Chandra who reached the ICU and after enquiring with the ICU staff Dr. Chamdra searched for Raja sab combing the entire RIMS but could not find him. Mittal rose from his seat in shock and sat down with heavy heart he gulped a glass of water and said DGP you are literally killing me am I your enemy and without any further utterance he said come let's go to home minister he enquired about the case status and both came down to ministers secretariat as usual ministers reception was crowded people were waiting for his audience, without waiting for any response from PA both the officers entered home ministers chamber, around 60 years medium built tall elderly gentlemen grey hairs sporting French cut beard fair complexion was in traditional Indian attire seated upon the chair interacting with a group of persons of age group between 30....and 50...occupying chairs opposite to him minster was assuring the group with a smile that action will be initiated immediately group left after reconfirming ministers assurance. Looking at DGP and after responding to his protocol, minister said yes gentlemen what's the purpose of your visit he enquired with Mittal, hesitatingly Mittal gave a brief account of Raja sab missing from hospital bed... minister rose from his seat in shock said OMG what is this new unpleasant development, advising both the visitors to be seated in anteroom he called his PA and said no phone calls and no visitors for 30 minutes from now and please send coffee for three with snacks. PA left minister entered the room, all the three were silent for some time later minister addressing DGP said department is responsible for Raja sabs missing without denying the accusation DGP said sir not only our department but in spite of RIMS having a very good security cover this incident has happened. Raja sab is gone unnoticed. Your admitting error will not relieve you from your utter negligence which will definitely prove costly for you and your department DGP in reply said sir still we have sufficient time to reach the deadline of 72 hours. So till such time please refrain from ifs and buts. The moment DGP stopped, the minister shot back. Suppose if you fail to live up to the expectations at the end of 72 hours then what next...DGP said I will forward my resignation letter to you. Same moment a gentle knock on the door and PA entered with the office assistant following with a tray containing a drinking water bottle, three empty glasses, coffee pot empty cups and snacks. Keeping the tray upon the table they left. Minister sipping coffee expressing his anguish said this unpleasant development will not go easy with my higher up's Raja sab is not an ordinary figure media will blow up the issue to extreme and people at the helm of affairs one above the other will play football with the subordinates, you people are having no idea how opposition will take the advantage of the happenings. Friends, you have informed me of the unpleasant incident and now you are free as the ball is in my court now. OMG how I am going to face my bosses, it is a million-dollar question. And God only knows Raja sab is alive or dead and if he is alive what could be the demand of kidnappers expressing his numerous doubts minister looked pale and helpless, through his appearance it was evident that he was scared of imagining his meeting with his bosses. DGP visualizing the minister's situation said minister sir Raja sab is definitely alive moreover kidnappers any move will land them in trouble and I am confident kidnapper will come out with his demand very leisurely after taking in account the police action enabling him/her to proceed with their plan behind kidnap. Minister shook his head indicating confused acceptance. Assessing ministers' displeasure DGP said sir be rest assured police has another 48 hours to submit our report. So, this is a saving point for you. Please tell your higher ups that you have given 48 hours with strict orders to comb north east west south and to come out with positive results within the expiry of deadline of 48 hours and I am confident Sir police will touch the bottom positively, in case if police fails to live up to the expectations then please handover the case to other central investigation agencies. Minister gave a sigh of relief and said yes, your statement sounds effective. OK gentlemen then let's disperse. I will have to inform my CM sir of the latest development. All came out of anteroom and bidding goodbye to minister Mr. Mittal and DGP came out to parking and parted in their respective vehicles.

Chapter - 9

The next morning...at PARADISE as usual at sunrise the inmates were on their move, PARADISE was busy with hectic activity as the last night's incident spread like wildfire throughout the city and media coverage gave the incident an added publicity nationwide. Well-wishers residing nearby thronged the Paradise and people from far and wide were taking the updates over phone. Staff was busy answering phone calls. Police had a hectic time in controlling the mob trying to enter Paradise. PA Rajiv on the advice of the Police commissioner installed a public address system at Paradise and was replying to their queries. Gradually the situation was returning to normalcy.

Dilip Kumar called Kishore and enquired about his position he said he is at Paradise and gave a live commentary of the situation at PARADISE, Dilip asked him whether he has taken the list of people who were invited to the party at Paradise and advised him to come with list to Dream House. accordingly Kishore reached and handed over the list to Dilip Kumar going through the list he enquired any particular person to be taken as suspect to which Kishore, gave the detail account of his interaction with Rajiv Dhawan and said as per PA Rajiv one real-estate agent Albert is said to be a troublesome shooter. a real estate agent constantly pressurizing Raja sab to sell a property which is existing in city outskirts and is around 15 acres. Raja sab is well aware of this and every time whenever Albert visits for the purpose Raja sab point blank refuses to oblige, still he keeps coming twice a week. Raja sab could have banned his entry but by nature he is never harsh to anyone, never speaks harshly and with a smile keeps denying what he doesn't like. He never loses his cool and always politely expresses his mind. And Rajiv Dhawan further added that Raja sabs younger brother Raja Denanath is one more character who is a very repulsive soul, Raja sab dislikes him for his lavish lethargy, indiscipline, immoral lifestyle and his attitude and very specifically his behavior towards staff. He has only one son who is post graduate in commerce and just one year younger to Prince, Jack took out a visiting card of Dinanath and gave it to Dilip kumar which he received from Rajiv, he requested not to disclose his name and also stated that he personally don't like him the reason is he wants Raja sab to give baby Meena in marriage to his son, who is unworthy for baby Meena. He keeps on visiting every now and then with the same proposal and Raja sab keeps on rejecting the proposal, more than this I could not gather anything more, but I have one doubt after going through the CCTV footage I noticed one lady below fifty's but above forty was trying to move close to Raja sab and Raja sab was seen to be very cordial to her.

Dilip Kumar quietly listened to Kishore and without passing any comment said come let's check Albert I know him and both came out.

It was evening 5 pm Dilip Kumar made a call to Albert and said I am coming to your place please be available, also declared the purpose of his visit and took out Willys jeep Dilip Kumar on the wheel drove towards the industrial area. Albert's house was in an industrial area. The unique part of this area is on one side of the 40 feet wide road is residential area and the other side of the road is industrial zone and majority of the industrialists having their establishments in this industrial zone have their residence here. After twenty minutes nonstop driving Dilip on reaching industrial area stopped at Alberts residence 'Lake view villa' it was a beautiful villa type house having a small garden full of flowery and decorative plants on either side of the path way leading to main entrance, pointing out at the nameplate Kishore said it is lake view villa but there is no lake nearby, Dilip with a smile said Kishore most probably you have not gone around the area my dear friend there is a lake behind those hillocks and government intends to develop it into a tourist spot it is full of greenery, water body and mountains you visit the area and you will fall in love and will like to stay there for a long time, Kishore just shrugged his shoulders.

At entrance in portico stood a middle aged man in black jeans and Blue T shirt having French cut beard must be around fifty years came hurriedly to receive Dilip Kumar, both shook hands later Dilip Kumar introduced Kishore to him he is Mr. Albert D'Souza, a realtor by profession. After a formal introduction Dilip said to Mr. Albert who all are keen to buy the farm house of Raja sab can you give me details and are you also a contender. Albert replying in negative pulled out a piece of paper from his trousers pocket and gave it to Dilip Kumar & said the moment you told me that you wish to know how many people are interested in buying the 15 acres of farm house situated at 40 kms out of city beyond international airport I immediately prepared the list and Sir for your information the parcel of land is beyond my reach so I have given up but I am trying for others on a lucrative commission. Dilip took the list from Albert and thanked him, called off the meeting and came down to the car, took a seat next to the driver advising Kishore to take the wheel and said let's have dinner in a hotel of your choice. Kishore giving a smile said thank God you also feel hungry my workaholic boss. Anyway, boss, why have you come so urgently to Albert as if something important will go out of hand? Staring at Kishore replying to his query Dilip said I think you have not followed DGPs instructions. He wants to report in two days' time and he is a very strict person with regards to work, he neither goes on leave nor allows anyone to go on leave except on reasonable grounds. To help you I have come with you and we have achieved a lot. Jack drove straight to hotel imperial, a nice five star lovable place built in Italian style equipped with the latest modern technology a little far from human jungle and sound pollution. Promoters did their best to give the hotel a love at first sight look, traditional Indian style welcome service at entrance by handsome and beautiful male and female staff, decent looking and neatly uniformed staff. Hotel had guests from all walks of life and from overseas too. Unique selling point of the hotel was the helicopter service free lift from airport to hotel and back to airport. Imperial was full with guests. Dilip Kumar and Kishore reached the hotel without wasting time and came down to the restaurant section. Both were guided to a two-seater corner table. Kishore was a regular client and staff was well acquainted with him. Kishore after confirming with Dilip Kumar placed an order for Indian food which was served hot in fifteen minutes, meanwhile both freshen up and without any talks finished their food and left the hotel, came back to the car and reached back home. During the journey Dilip was busy making and receiving phone calls. He was telling someone on the other side Yes I know I was expecting this even now I am being followed in fact the trail started from Alberts residence. Anyway, you keep a track and now I am on my way back to my dream house and disconnected. Jack turning to Dilip Kumar said we were being followed, you did not alert me. Dilip with a smile said my dear JACK of all trade trailing started from Alberts residence so in order to cross check and confirm my doubt we took a dinner break. And now I am confident we are on the right path, please tell me something in detail to which Dilip Kumar said don't jump to conclusions wait and see, Willys jeep reached dream house both left the vehicle in portico and went inside, Vehicle was parked in garage by staff member of dream house.

Chapter - 10

Next day 8.30 am at Dream House, Crime bureau Chief Dilip Kumar was interacting with Detective Inspector KISHORE submitting Paradise report Kishore stated that, I noticed that KAMINI was trying to move close to Raja sab and in turn Raja sab was probably enjoying her company, not even once Raja sab attempted to avoid her. Dilip smiled at Kishores remarks and said Good observation Kishore,

Kishore continuing said I have seen CCTV footage and found nothing suspicious except one point that Ms KAMINI, the so called social worker was seen with Raja sab moving very closely and even Raja sab was cordially receiving her but Albert was greeted half-heartedly that to in presence of Ms KAMINI in the footage it was appearing as if he was hurt. And after a few minutes he was seen leaving PARADISE.

Kishore further stated that when he visited Paradise and sought Ms Meena's audience through PA Rajiv he was called to the main building. PA Rajiv guided him into PARADISE main building and was seated in a magnificent hall, on entering hall he was excited on seeing history on walls...hall was full of portraits of ancestors of Raja sab who ruled the country once upon a time, portraits of other kings and Britishers who once ruled the nation what all he read in history was speaking to him through pictures displayed on the walls. I was very much impressed after witnessing a lively well placed pictures gallery and amusement ended on the entry of Ms Meena. Welcoming greetings she enquired the purpose of my visit, PA Rajiv was also present in the hall and before I could state the purpose of my visit, I heard someone inside scolding, someone throwing utensils and shouting at the top of his voice, I realized it was Prince releasing his anger. While I was enquiring about the staff, Meena and Rajiv were speechless. They were just looking at one another, by their facial expressions it was evident that they were repenting for calling me into the main building. Dilip just shook his head in acceptance. He further added that Raja sabs driver Sandeep returned from his village and joined duty, i casually spoke to him that fellow seems to be too attached to Raja sab and was literally crying while answering my questions, best example of dedication devotion and die hard employee, Dilip was Intensely listening to Kishore said now you keep a watch on Albert for 24 hours without even a wink of sleep .

And later on we will focus on Kamini. Now you have to follow Albert for 24 hours night and day and you must be at his residence. Come what may I need minute to minute report for night surveillance you can befriend a tea stall exactly opposite to Albert's house. You make a place for yourself by befriending the stall owner and in a simple make up presenting yourself in your forties. You migrated to the city from a nearby neighboring village as agriculture is not yielding required income and your family is large, rest you know how to handle. Please note you are supposed to keep a watch on movements of Albert visitors and any other suspicious activity, refrain from visiting Albert's place let anything happen there, just be a silent spectator. Please use your mobile sparingly, no high end mobile, better use an ordinary mobile. Now make a move from today 10 am you must be on job as Alberts day starts from 11 am but their day ends after midnight.

Kishore hurriedly came out and entered the lab in the dream house and came out after 30 minutes in a simple getup appearing as a middle-aged peasant and taking a lift from one of the dream house staff he reached the industrial area with a small basket in hand containing roasted nuts and grams. Sending back the vehicle he walked down and reached the tea stall, which was a small but neat and clean eatery serving hot drinks, biscuits, packed hot items, bisleri water bottles, cool drinks and other general items like mobile recharge, stationery items and packed lunch packets but in limited numbers. Person on the counter was a middle aged man with a smiling face a little heavy possessing extra pounds of flesh upon body. At a glance Kishore assessed him as a soft going person. As it was self service Kishore bought a cup of strong tea, a symbolic item to indicate that he is a villager. His plan worked and the person at the counter introduced himself as Ramesh, owner of the stall and enquired where the brother where are you from. A simple query was enough for Kishore to make a place in Ramesh's soft corner and he narrated a fictitious emotional tale of a large family dry fields and meager earnings as a result he is out to earn for survival, Ramesh was moved by his tale and consoling him said long ago once upon a time I was like you wandering all alone no support but for you I am here be sure you will settle very soon in your life. Kishore thanked him for his affectionate attitude. Ramesh offered him tea and advised him to sit on that bench placed by the side of the tea stall and expect customers. Thanking Ramesh, he got busy... As per Dilip Kumar's instructions busy keeping a strict vigil on the incoming and outgoing people from Albert's lake view residence, Albert was very popular in his line of activity enjoying good rapport with clients and allied departments. He was known as a "man of word" come what may and never fails in his commitment, He was one of the invitees at Raja sab recent party, hence his name was in suspect list.

Grant road a busy posh residential area in northern side surrounded by beautiful natural landscape a chain of small hills with greenery everywhere—state and central government are planning to make it a tourist spot which is in pipeline from a very long time as there is a beautiful blue water lake surrounded by these hillocks and the presence of all these three (hills, greenery, lake) gives the area a picturesque look and of course enhancing the demand and land value beyond the reach of rich middle class only the richest from the rich community can conveniently afford to own the prime place which was directly under the control of STATE DEVELOPMENT CORPORATION (SDC) — Industrial area has access for abundant water, so all in all grant road area is well developed by class people all independent villas beautiful houses, roads, playground for children and opposite to the industrial area richest of rich community who could comfortably own the choicest place and peace loving people were dwelling in their beautiful eye-catching well planned well-built cottage's, people who visit the city do visit this area to enjoy sightseeing.. The large industrial /commercial area fully occupied with nonpolluting industries in between the residential area and commercial area is a

40 feet wide road connecting the state highway taking to neighboring states—And on the top of it many residents of this area are also industry owners. Albert's residence existed near to the main road having two side roads, high boundary walls, huge iron gate with two security guards guarding the entrance the main building standing around 25 meters away from the main gate, wide pathway leading to the main building entrance either side trees and well maintained garden. Kishore was on duty with a big hand basket, the upper cover of the basket resembling like a tray having 3 inches depth divided into two portions filled with peanuts and fried yellow grams, since morning dressed up in formal kurta pajama, big mustache black and white a wrinkle or two on the face giving an appearance of a middle aged old man, tired looks, shoulders down and bent to some extent, this was Kishore, he kept his basket near the bench and relaxed sipping his tea.

Later Ramesh came down to Kishore and giving a detailed account of his family said, we are family of 7 elders and 5 children—aged old parents, my father's divorced sister with son my younger brother (Rajesh) I am the elder son of my parents we both the brothers have 2 children each and I am the head of the family – I take care of morning business from 7 am to 8 pm and Rajesh looks after night business 8 pm to 8 am—being in industrial area and on state highway we have good business and we all are happy on this tea stall we have purchased a house in nearby interior middle class area and we have purchased two motorcycles and our children are studying in community school existing in our locality.

Kishore said I am delighted to meet you. You are a very good gentleman, God bless you. Ramesh enquired How about your nights where you are sleeping, Kishore with a smile pointing out at sky said care of God. Ramesh laughing said Oh don't worry now I will introduce you to Rajesh and at night you can sleep behind the tea stall there is one cot.

Kishore thanking him said so kind of you Ramesh, Oh no it's my duty as a human, about your dinner, you can have it here only if you don't have money no problem pay later.

Acknowledging Ramesh's kindness Kishore said I have no words to thank you, Almighty God is very merciful upon me, he has sent an angel for my help in you in this strange surroundings.

Ramesh just laughed and smiled and got busy in his routine – mean while assistant purchased tea and biscuits and murmured – fellow this is your destiny having pocket full of money but you can't buy any good food so survive on tea biscuits, sipping tea and biscuits he was continuously watching movements of people coming and going out of Albert's gate, till 2 pm nothing abnormal was seen but after 2 pm Kishore noticed one sky blue Innova bearing number DLB3473 entering the gate two persons on the back seat and a familiar face behind the steering – Kishore going down the memory lane recollected he was MOHAN VERMA— senior council of Raja sab why he is at suspect Albert along with two other strangers—As he could not solve the mystery, decided to inform the same to Dilip Kumar— he told Ramesh, Brother I will make a call to my brother to inform him my where abouts and will be back in few minutes, please take care of my basket and after walking away from the spot—he took out his phone called Dilip Kumar and informed him the developments, Dilip said—Good job be alert and also note the timings of entry and exit and also note how many went inside and how many came out.

:Can I call off the mission asked Kishore as we have got the lead, Dilip replied Don't be foolish it's just a radical information, go back and keep a watch till I call you back no more questions over and out keep your cell on vibration, disconnecting the call Kishore came back to the spot had tea and snacks at Ramesh – time was running out it was evening sunset industries first shift came to an end – Kishore saw a visitor at the gate with parcel -it was a courier boy – labors after completing their shift started coming out and area became crowdy buzzing of horns and movement of two-three and four wheelers—surrounding was too noisy and in this noisy atmosphere assistant heard three gunshot sounds one after another from the residence under surveillance, Kishore was confused what to do – whether to run inside house or to wait and watch finally he decided to wait and watch – meanwhile he saw Ramesh going to the scene of crime—After a little while he saw the police arrived on the spot—After one hour Kishore saw police shifting a body draped in cloth and in another fifteen minutes everything was quiet and normal as if nothing has happened—Ramesh was back from the crime scene and he narrated the happenings at the crime scene, with a grim face and faulting the society said What is happening to the society its broad day light murder right under the nose of two security guards – the security guards were found unconscious in their cabin assassin came walking entered the house and shot the house owner and vanished in the industrial crowd, it all happened in a fraction of few seconds and none could give any clue to the police-Kishore enquired Who has been murdered and who was the visitor

Ramesh said it was realator Albert and the victims house maid said he brought some small parcel and after handing of the parcel while he (visitor) was taking sir's signature maid left the room and went upstairs to take up the leftover cleaning work and on hearing the gunshots by the time she came down to the hall no one was there and sir was lying in the pool of blood—she started screaming – The gardener an old man in 60's who stays in a room behind the main building entered hearing her screams and he called the police-

Kishore then asked What about the security guards did they inform you of anything?

No brother, security guards were found unconscious in their room and after bringing them to conscious by police they stated that visitor was a stranger for them and wanted to give the parcel to the addressee in person–

Then how come both were found unconscious enquired Kishore to which Ramesh said I don't know and added brother, the assassin was very smart, it seems the two guards went inside the security room, along with the visitor and head guard spoke to their boss on intercom and informed him that courier boy has come with a parcel for him and insists to hand over to him in person, Albert advised the guard to send him – before entering the house visitor said he wish to keep his courier bag there in the security room so guard called the senior in to the cabin- guards bent to unzip and check the bag inside suddenly the visitor pumped spray and both fell unconscious seems they didn't see what was in the bag

Kishore expressed that the police can find out with the courier company after checking the parcel.

Ramesh with a smile said Brother, assassin is very smart he delivered an empty box wrapped in glossy color paper with only the victim's address and sender's address is not there and there is no paper

Oh quite smart killer, let's leave this topic, friend police will do their job sooner or later they will catch the culprit stated Kishore.

There are two CCTV cameras one is on the entrance at the gate and second one at portico stated Ramesh and added, police has got anything from that I don't know—anyway brother my duty time is over—my brother Rajesh will come at any moment, I will introduce him to you—same moment Rajesh landed, after completing change over formalities-Ramesh introducing Kishore to Rajesh—strictly advised him to be good counsel, he will stay here tonight and also advised Rajesh to dine together and he left bidding goodbye to both.

Kishore and Rajesh had a casual discussion and over dinner, Assistant gave Rajesh a brief account of the crime to which Rajesh responded very sordidly and commented So you sow though you reap –brother he paid for his sins Why do you say like that remarked Kishore. Brother he was a very wicked man—ladies and suspicious persons used to visit him very frequently.

Kishore said Ladies visiting is common in society but suspicious persons visiting, what makes you say so

Rajesh said Brother, first of all good people visit day time, even bad people visit daytime but bad people only visit late nights and I have seen one person visiting very recurrently, he comes sometimes in car, sometimes on two wheeler, sometimes in a group of one or more and sometimes alone—always I have seen him in black dress head covered with cap, beard and mask on face.

Do you have any idea what was the business of the deceaseds. No idea brother asserted Rajesh.

Having done with the dinner Kishore dog tired stretched his legs on the cot and unknowingly and unintentionally fell asleep. Suddenly he woke up as if someone is shaking him, yes it was his mobile on vibration, he took out the phone and saw it was a message from Dilip Kumar to abort the mission and meet him in the office tomorrow morning – Next day Kishore bidding goodbye to Ramesh for his hospitality said I will try my luck for good sales somewhere in school zones—Ramesh approved his decision and both bidding emotional good bye parted.

Chapter - 11

KAMINI

Settling down upon the chair Dilip Kumar called Kishore enquired him his position, Kishore replied he is in PARADISE and going through CCTV footage. Dilip advised him to reach office after he is done and disconnected. At 6 pm Kishore knocking Dilip's door entered found him busy in file. Taking a seat he said boss forensic report has come and here it is pulling out one envelope he handed over the same to Dilip Kumar and said I have seen CCTV footage at Paradise and found nothing suspicious except one point that Ms KAMINI around 45 years smart and good looking attractive personality well dressed, the so called social worker was seen with Raja sab moving very closely and even Raja sab was cordially receiving her but Albert was greeted half-heartedly that to in presence of Ms KAMINI in the footage it was appearing as if he was hurt. Dilip Kumar said close Albert file he is no more now you concentrate and focus on KAMINI, you have to follow Ms KAMINI for 24 hours night and day you must be her shadow come what may I need her minute to minute report for night surveillance you can take the help of area patrol disclosing them that subject KAMINI is very important and you want them to be very cautious.

Next day on Dilip Kumars advise from 8 am Kishore was on assignment of following Ms KAMINI she was residing in a higher middle class colony well designed independent houses every house was different from other house in coloring the structures and it gave a pleasant look to the new comer....a multicolor colony well maintained by the colony association, road side garden, playground for children and a park spread in one acre of land having beautiful ornamental plants, flowery plants a circular walking path around two miles, with drinking water facility and seating arrangements everywhere for visitors, Kishore was keenly observing all these facilities provided to the residents and colony was named "rainbow residency" this name was because of multicolor structures, Rainbow residency was situated just two kilometers away from madding crowd in a quite peaceful atmosphere and to left was approach road to state highway which was 10 kms away from national highway, Kishore parking his Willys jeep a little away from KAMINI's residence which was near to the park, adjusted his rearview mirror and now he could distinctly keep an eye on her main entrance he took out today's newspaper and was pretending to be busy reading newspaper but in reality Kishore's eyes were on rear view mirror of jeep watching the main entrance of KAMINIs residence. Waiting period for Kishore ended at 9 am KAMINI clad in smooth Bengal handloom light grey color saree emerged from her residence driving her SWIFT blue metallic air conditioned car. Jeep , maintaining a distance, was following the Swift car which after taking the main road traveling for around 30 minutes entering city limits stopped in front of the state bank. Ms KAMINI coming out of the car went inside the bank and returned after 30 minutes. Again Swift was on the road heading towards busy commercial area of city called Silver Jubilee market commonly known as SJ market which was established before independence in the heart of the city trading only in precious metal and more particularly dealing in silver hence the name silver jubilee market was christened in those days. Here Kishore following KAMINI stopped his jeep at a distance and he saw a young man in thirty's neatly dressed in white shirt and sky blue trousers sporting full face beard carrying a big cartoon came near KAMINIs car she got down from her car and moved a side enabling the person carrying cardboard cartoon to keep the box in the car keeping the box in the car he went away. Now Swift was on the move from one road to another taking turn after turn and at last entering a slum area, Parking her car near a community welfare hall she went inside Kishore was in his jeep only and stopped near a small shop got down and reaching the shop purchased salt biscuits and came back to jeep. It was 11 am and Kishore was yet to take his breakfast and sensing he delay he started consuming biscuits and after throwing away the empty biscuit cover he again visited shop and purchased a 500 ml soft drink a fruit juice bottle and to buy time he advised the shopkeeper to chill the bottle and he initiated casual talks beginning with his sales and other allied facilities availability, water supply power supply and then came down to the point purpose of community welfare center. To which shopkeeper said for colony meetings and if any government schemes they will be held here only any small get together will be take place here only and any other important meeting event medical camps and so on.

Kishore appreciating the move asked any event going presently he said yes sir a social worker from city Ms DEVI is a regular visitor every fortnight and she comes with cartoon full of certain items and distribute them among ladies and go away. From last few year she has been a regular visitor every month on the second Saturday and last Saturday from 11 am till 1 pm she will be here only. Kishore looked at his watch it was 12.15 pm, still nearly an hour left over. He cursed himself so deeply immersed in thoughts cursing the surveillance job he came out of day dream when he heard shopkeeper calling him with the juice bottle in his hand glancing at the watch taking the bottle in his hand, he advised the shopkeeper to keep it again for few more minutes and around 01.05 noon he took the juice bottle which was too chilled he returned to his jeep and sat down and keeping himself busy over phone started sipping juice gradually. Kishore's eyes were on the main entrance of community hall and around 1.15 pm he saw Ms KAMINI coming out headed straight to her car and again the car was on the main road in a couple of minutes.

This time Swift going through posh city roads entered a 4 star hotel Royal resort after leaving the car in portico. She left the keys in the car for the hotel guide to park the car in the valet parking lot. Ms KAMINI entered the hall and after looking at her wrist watch she settled in the waiting lounge. Kishore followed her into the hall and internally thanked her for taking a break in this hotel Kishore was a known figure in city's posh hotels...here also he was not a new face. He was also watching KAMINI, constantly she was looking at the wall clock again and again it was appearing as if she was waiting for someone. Around 2.30 pm three people aged between 30 and 35 entered and walked straight to Ms KAMINI and settled on the sofa opposite to her. She pointing out at the wall clock was expressing her unhappiness for their late entry later Ms KAMINI with the group was busy in discussions it was appearing as if she was explaining something important to them and they were nodding their head in acceptance, Later all of them left their seats and entered hotels dining hall upon a table of four Kishore luckily could get a vacant seat just behind them sitting there he could conveniently hear them noticeably. They placed their order and were busy in general talks, at one point the so-called gang leader said madam police is on high alert and we have to be very cautious as police is yet to gain a breakthrough in Raja sab issue, to which Ms KAMINI replied don't worry you all will go unnoticed. Later Food was served and during food they quietly finished their food and over soft drinks one of them appearing to be gang leader their leader asked Madam last question we will observe the happenings then we will take action, hope you don't mind in reply Ms KAMININ said take a day or two makes no difference but the solution should be sustainable, as directed later she gave them a bundle of currency notes and they left. Ms KAMINI after clearing the food bill came out, a valet parking guide brought the car and within minutes her swift was rolling out of Royal Resort. Kishore who was out of the dining hall before

Ms KAMINI and her associates were out, was seated in the waiting lounge and when those three associates of Ms KAMINI came out he clicked their picture on his mobile without being noticed. And now he was following Ms KAMINI again clock was striking 5 pm and Ms KAMINIs car was on the busy road negotiating turns and traffic and finally the driving came to an end and the car was entering PARADISE After Kamini's car entering PARADISE Kishore did not go inside but he stopped a little away from PARADISE entrance and made a call to headquarters and advised his assistant Rajesh sub inspector rank officer to reach paradise and after his arrival in 20 minutes he advised Rajesh to follow KAMINI who is in PARADISE and instructed to follow her till she is back home and to call him before calling off the day. It was 6 pm Kishore left the spot. Rajesh reached PARADISE on his official motorcycle in civil dress, he was SI and was recently transferred from law and order department to crime department on promotion from ASI to SI, he was young smart enthusiastic law graduate and was eagerly trying to gain recognition in the department.

And the assignment given by Kishore was like dream come true for him. Around 6.45 pm KAMINIs car came out of PARADISE on the road and she was very casually driving as if she was not in a hurry. The car came out of the city and proceeded straight to Rainbow residency and reaching her residence KAMINI parked her car and called off the day. Rajesh passed on the information to Kishore and he advised him to wait for the reliever and call of the day thereafter. In twenty minutes, time night patrol van came over there and Rajesh gave them the charge and left.

Chapter - 12

Dilip Kumar and Kishore reached office clock was striking 9 am, When they entered office Dilip Kumar's mobile started ringing he responded to the call, on the other side it was his personnel staff, after few minutes Dilip disconnected and turning to Kishore said, the assassin who killed Albert, has been identified and when our people went to nab him he was found dead in his room—throat slit open using sharp edge doctor's knife said Dilip Kumar.

Anything found in the room during search enquired Kishore

Nothing found, police are still there conducting searches, come let's join them asserted Dilip.

Accordingly both came out of office and boarded Scorpio—Officer on the wheel car came out on the clean—cement road and headed towards northern part of the city which is thickly populated with upper and lower middle class people—after entering the colony called MS colony (Modern Society colony)—a police escort was waiting at the entrance to receive the officials—Police vehicle led the Scorpio to the crime scene after going through lanes by lanes—assassin was residing in a one bedroom hall kitchen flat semi furnished—just a cot and a sofa set with central table fan walls naked no posters and photos, one small trolley bag containing a couple of dresses, a night dress, tooth brush, paste, soap, towel, glass and plates, small fridge containing only drinking water bottles, bread, butter, jam. That's all nothing more than this. After a detail study of the crime scene Dilip said this assassin was not in a hurry, moreover this is a temporary hide out he is not from this area—Dilip after a glance of the room interacting with the Investigating Officer asked who gave you the information regards to the dead body, to which in reply Investigating Officer pointed out at one elderly person standing in one corner Investigating Officer said his name is Balram from northern part of the country and he is watch man of this complex, Anything more Yes sir as per Balram the victim came to him in search of a rented accommodation in reply Balram informed him that this flat has been sold out yesterday and the purchaser is planning to renovate the interiors painting and other allied changes and the victim said he is a painter by profession and has come from a village to eke out living believing him Balram gave him new owner Sunder Sohanlals number. More than this he has no information. Dilip advised Kishore to take down the number of Sunder Sabarwal and enquire with him. Dilip advised the Investigating Officer to keep him informed if any new development occurs.

Dilip along with Kishore came out and came down to parking advised Kishore to look for the two wheeler used by the victim, after looking around Kishore came and said the parking space allotted to the flat is vacant no vehicle is there.

I am sure you have taken the flat ownership details Dilip enquired with Kishore and he said Yes sir I knew you will ask for this so I have details -it belongs to Sohanlal tours and travels and manpower agents, their office is situated at RP Road. Good job now kindly get down at any convenient point and get me the details of this tour and travel agent, find out the link between assassin and Sohanlal group and reach me as soon as possible, with these instructions Dilip stopped Scorpio and dropped Kishore at RP road Scorpio zoomed away. -Kishore from there he walked down to the Sohanlal tours and travels as it was nearby, reaching the spot he entered the office, a well lit premises having 3 cabins, waiting hall, reception three female clerks, one male office assistant- total five staff members. Founder chairman was available in the office-Kishore met receptionist and seeking an audience with the chairman settled on a sofa set –after 10 minutes wait Kishore was led into chairman's chambers, he saw a senior citizen in traditional Indian attire neatly dressed, semi-bald, white hairs, normal built clean shave must be around 60+, smiling face was the attraction point on his face—introducing himself Kishore explained the purpose of his visit after exchanging pleasantries – he inquired about the flat—and showing the picture of the murdered assassin enquired, police found dead body of this person in your flat - was he your tenant.

Sabarwal Pressing the call bell replying to assistant said sir please wait I will give you details same moment office boy entered chairman's cabin—Sabarwal called for Anita, office administrative head, after few seconds knocking the door a thin skinny fair good looking girl of 27-28 years entered in the chamber followed by office boy with a tray containing tea pot and water bottle with two empty glasses and two cups—while office boy was making tea Sabarwal turning to Anita pointing out at Kishore said he is police inspector crimes department and it seems that police found a dead body in one flat at RP road, in MS Colony, are we in anyway related to the property, I don't remember of owning a property in that area

Anita replying said Actually CEO sir recently purchased the property with an intention to expand the business in man power supplying as the area has potential being a middle class colony and people of that area are not satisfied with the two existing officers in that area – last two months back a group of people called upon CEO sir and requested to open an office in that area.

Then why was I not informed, and questioned Sabarwal?

Sir actually honored the request of the visitors CEO sir surveyed the area and market and negotiated a property last month for office purpose and was planning to open the office on any auspicious day after doing renovation works declared Anita.

Cutting Anita's explanation Sabarwal said, I should have been informed of the entire planning

That's what sir CEO sir wanted to inform you and take you to the office after renovation—Just keep quiet and said Where is CEO send him, CEO sir has not yet come sir she said

Sabarwal: Oh my God it's half day gone and he is yet to come, CEO sir called and informed that he will visit RPO office in connection with immigration check issue of two clients –

Sabarwal said Ok you can go, please send him in, the moment he arrives—giving a positive reply Anita came out of chairman's chambers.

listening to the conversation of boss and staff silently Kishore broke his silence and enquired about CEO

Sabarwal replied, "The CEO is my eldest son who completed his engineering and is associated with me from the past two years looking after manpower providing—in fact he started this section – earlier we were just ticketing and travel agents as I am aging he is looking after the entire business. Ok ok when can I meet him, meeting is important said Kishore.

I will just call him and confirm – said Sabarwal and over intercom advised Anita to confirm CEOs whereabouts and ask him to reach office immediately. Anita entered the chamber and informed the CEO is on the way. Sabarwal turning to Kishore asked, is it ok sir

Kishore nodded his head in acceptance, Sabarwal urged upon his son to come down as soon as possible and disconnected the call.

The next 20 minutes were killed with one more cup of tea and before the end of 20 minutes a smart young man with a well built personality dressed up in matching attire tall and very fair entered the chamber. After a casual introduction the CEO –name Mohanlal was shown the photo of deceased and he said no sir he is a stranger to me in fact I have called for office renovation and kept the keys with the watchman of the complex—turning to his father he continuing said daddy office is located on the ground floor, its centrally located with all amenities so I took over. In fact I wanted to show you after renovation—actually it's for my younger brother Sohanlal, I planned to open a branch as he is going to complete his degree this year

Sabarawal patiently listening to his son said, everything is ok but what you have to say about this dead body—

Mohanlal said Dad I am ignorant and I have not taken the keys and possession of the flat, keys are kept with the watchman to show the flat to the people visiting for renovation—

Kishore got up and while leaving the office advised Mohanlal not to go out of the city without permission and to cooperate with the police—From there hiring a taxi he reached headquarters. Dilip Kumar was not in the office, Kishore called him and in a sarcastic tone asked for his next assignment, on the other side Dilip Kumar laughing to his content said my dear detective, collect the full report of Kamini from the night duty surveillance and make a complete report and expect me at Dream House after dinner and disconnected.

<h1 style="text-align:center">Chapter - 13</h1>

Kishore after coming out from Sohanlal Travels hiring a taxi reached back to Dream house. It was lovely cool evening, Kishore having relaxed for a long decided to meet his only true friend Rohit Saxsena accordingly after 40 minutes Kishore was on the road heading towards hotel King Palace, dressed elegantly reached hotel KING PALACE a clean maintaining good hygiene a five star hotel very much in the heart of the city, usually King Palace attracts large customers because the price tag of eatables, comparatively to other star hotels KING PALACE was with in reach of a middle class group and on account of this people friendly policy of the management hotel is always crowded.

As usual hotel was crowdy and hardly there was any table left unoccupied but Kishore was least bothered as he was confident that his friend Rohit Saxsena the only son of a richest high profile industrialist Raj Saxsena an MBA graduate who spares hardly a couple of hours to look after his father's business and most of the time he loves sleeping for hours, going out on a long drive and visiting hotels and he loves to be called Rocky in friend circle. And King Palace was Rocky's choicest hotel. Kishore came down straight to Rocky around 29 years. A well-built handsome young man, very fair and tall in clean shave neatly dressed was on the table flirting with two young women in their 20's. On seeing Kishore, he was excited and said welcome my dear James bond, how are you after a long time. On Rocky's signal both the girls left. Kishore pointing out at girls said fellow you are not bored with this daily money minded call girls flirting with you just for your money. Rocky laughing wholeheartedly said my dear friend, do you think I am a fool no my friend I am fully aware that these girls are out for a earning and indirectly I help them by just flirting with them and not subjecting them to physical cruelty and these girls feel safe profitable and happy in my company. Kishore realized Rocky was absolutely correct hence not discussing further on the subject he said, anyways what's going on any new worth mentioning incidence to share with me, Rocky said nothing specific but one evening as usual when the hall was pack one evening a couple aged between 30 ...... 35 good looking were guided by floor manager Joseph to my table I was sitting alone he requested me to accommodate them and they will leave after dinner. I obliged The couple had their dinner during dinner they did not speak but over coffee after dinner both were engulfed in serious discussions and subject was the attack on Raja sab I did not pay any attention as it was not topic of my interest but at one point I was forced to listen to their talks, Kishore asked what was the point of your attraction Rocky said male member was telling attack on Raja sab was false just to attract attention of his well-wishers and to gain sympathy to which lady said how do you justify your statement to which male said I have evidence to prove. At that time the waiter came with the bill, they paid the bill and left. That's all-Kishore enquired Rocky replied in positive. Rocky and Kishore enjoyed the orchestra ordering food and by the time they finished their food and ice cream it was 11 pm.

Rocky called for the bill and Joseph came with the bill while paying the bill Kishore enquired about the couple, he guided to Rocky's table to which he said sir they paid me a heavy four figures tip with a request to arrange them two seats for dinner. and more than this I know nothing about them. Kishore disposed of him and said Rocky they chose your table because they were aware of our friendship, anyways forget that anything important will surface automatically.

After paying bill Rocky and Kishore came out of King Palace and bidding goodbye parted in their vehicles Rocky zoomed out in his latest metallic blue color air conditioned Octiva. And Kishore in his Willys was in deep thought thinking about the couple on Rocky's table. Going little further he noticed one black sedan following him right from hotel King Palace To further confirm his doubt he came down to KAMINI's Rainbow residency and he saw patrol car in front of the main entrance facing standing on the road as if some road checking is in process, Kishore came down to patrol car and enquired about KAMINI they said she is at home only. Kishore advised them to keep a watch up till 7 am and then call off the day after receiving reliever. Patrol team accepted and Kishore was again on the road and Sedan was trailing behind maintaining a distance. Trailing was confirmed. After driving for 20 minutes his jeep halted in front of PARADISE main entrance. Since the attack on Raja sab a special police picket was guarding the PARADISE and its inmates. Kishore called the night duty staff they came and after a casual enquiry advising them to be alert, he started from PARADISE and drove back to DREAM HOUSE gate was opened and he parked his jeep and while going to main building entrance he saw Sedan zoomed away.

For Kishore the day was very hectic and Dilip Kumar was also not available. He was sure that Dilip Kumar would call him any moment and decided to take a nap to feel fresh for the next assignment, as a result after a change he fell on the bed and in minutes he was in deep slumber.

It was the mobile ring which woke him up answering the call before he said hello and it was Dilip Kumar on the other side who advised him to reach the office immediately and the call was disconnected. Halfheartedly Kishore left the bed and after 40 minutes left the house reluctantly. After the end of forty minutes Kishore was standing in front of Dilip Kumar, with a smile Dilip welcomed Kishore and asked how was your yesterday evening and what was your outcome of following KAMINI. you did a good job by seeking help from Rajesh and patrol good job now give me details what you have found out. Without replying to Dilip, Kishore said you called at a jet speed. I came running thinking something big has happened but here you are cooly enquiring about the trailing report. My dear friend every move in this case is very important to me whether KAMINI or anyone else, anyway keep a side your allegations and detail me what have you noticed and what is your reading about KAMINI, in reply Kishore gave the detail report and expressed that she might not be directly involved in the attack on Raja sab but I am confident she is helping the main conspirator, justifying his allegations he showed the photo of the three persons who met Kamini in hotel after seeing pictures keeping it a side Dilip asked what more, Kishore said Raja sab is in hospital his children are also busy out of PARADISE now tell me what was the purpose of her visiting PARADISE late evening hours. Dilip Kumar gave a smile and said good going, keep it up my friend.

Chapter - 14

Dog tired mentally and physically Commissioner of Police Karim Khan took just a sandwich and a glass of fresh juice for dinner and went to bed and he fell asleep instantly.

Sun was shining bright it was only 8 am but seeing the sunlight one could say it is around noon...mobile phone was ringing vigorously which woke up Police commissioner he immediately picked the receiver and was little alert as other side it was a call from DGP-Sharat Saxena and he advised police commissioner to reach PARADISE immediately. The Commissioner of police within a few minutes was in his official chauffeur driven car seated on the back seat...he took out his mobile and called Dilip Kumar the call was answered in two rings.. Commissioner of Police Karim Khan said where are you Dilip, twist after twist in Raja sabs case is nerve chilling and now, I am proceeding to PARADISE in response to DGPs call, and I am confident something very serious issue will greet me, from other end Dilip Kumar said Sir you reach the destination and I will join you soon.

At PARADISE the situation was very tense DGP was seated on a chair in one corner CoP went directly to DGP and he briefing CoP said on the city outskirts Raja sabs PA Rajiv Dhawan's car was found abandoned and his dead body was found near PARADISE...continuing DGP said incidence after incidence are compelling me to think that gulf between culprit and police is widening rather than police nearing the culmination. Commissioner was speechless and just nodded his head in affirmation. While both the top cops were busy in analyzing the occurrences right from the beginning the same moment Dilip Kumar entered in PARADISE joining DGP and police commissioner after formal protocol he enquired what exactly happened. And DGP in detail informed him that PAs dead body was found lying 100 meters away from PARADISE it was noticed by some passerby who informed the area patrol van which was stationed near by...patrolling staff were familiar with PA hence they called two PARADISE staff members to identify the body and after the staff replying in positive patrol team informed the control room and as the event is related to Raja sab control room informed me as a result we are here. One more information Raja sabs PAs dead body is found near paradise and his car abandoned near state highway almost city outskirts. What is your opinion regarding this current development Dilip Kumar. In reply Dilip enquiring that anyone has gone to inspect the car DGP said our highway patrol van is there only. Dilip Kumar asked for the body of PA and was told that after autopsy the body has been stored in a mortuary waiting for his son to arrive and conduct last rites. Commissioner informed that his son who is in Australia has been informed and he is arriving tomorrow for a couple of days and will go back permanently after conducting his fathers last rites. I pray God he should not come to me for any help, Dilip laughed a while and said nothing.

Dilip Kumar after a brief silence asked for the person who first saw the body and informed the police and in reply he was told that some unknown person on the way to his destination informed the police, the area police responded immediately and the station house officer who was familiar with PA immediately called the chief security and as a result we are here.

Dilip Kumar urged upon DGP and police commissioner for a visit to the spot where the PAs car is parked, DGP enquired anything specific to which Dilip Kumar said only after the inspection of the spot I can pass my remarks.

The three officers in DGPs car headed towards the spot. The scene of the crime where PAs car was parked on reaching the spot, Dilip Kumar made a thorough inspection every bit, he also took pictures of the car from different angles. it took nearly 30 minutes later all the three officers commenced their return journey towards headquarters, journey up till headquarters was very silent none of the three uttered a word after reaching police headquarters all the three settled in DGPs chambers and DGP called for tea and over a cup of tea Dilip Kumar said Sir whoever is the culprit did his best to misguide the police, DGP requested Dilip Kumar to complete his submission without break in one go justifying your allegations accusations and apprehensions Dilip Kumar going in detail said sir, whosoever the culprit is he committed a crime in haste, mentally he had no intentions of committing murder but was compelled to do so and in order to put the investigation on wrong path he left the car at highway and dropped the body near to PARADISE just to create thrill. DGP interrupting asked are you sure Dilip?"

With a simple smile Dilip said Sir first of all the position of the car indicates as if the person driving the car was following someone the driver had a confrontation with the person he was following this means, the driver of the car was familiar with the assassin and I am confident Sir the murder was absolutely unintentional. DGP and Commissioner both were appearing to be dumb and deaf characters after a few seconds both simultaneously questioned how are you so sure Dilip.

Dilip said Sir the positioning of the car was as if heading out of city but truth is that where the car stopped confrontation took place there only and most probably the victim was unknowingly attacked and blow was fatal and he lost his life here the culprit in panic left car in the opposite direction, the tyre marks and placement of the car proves my claims, and he dropped the body near Paradise to keep the police busy away from the car to be busy here with body, cross checking their assumptions. But his bad luck city patrol police found the body and the car was found by state highway patrol who through documents identified the owner and cross checked with the paradise again, a co incidence body was found first followed by detection of the car.

Dilip Kumar said sir Please give me just 24 hours and I will give you the culprit positively. DGP looked at Commissioner as if asking his opinion on Dilip kumar's request, realizing DGPs intentions Commissioner said to DGP sir we have 40 hours left giving 24 hours to Dilip will we will not lose anything on the contrary positively we will achieve some lead enabling us to pacify our heads. DGP nodded his head in acceptance of this, Dilip rose from his seat and left DGPs chamber.

After Dilip Kumar's exit DGP questioned the Commissioner, are you confident Dilip will keep up his assertion. Commissioner after a brief pause said, Sir I will enlighten you with few facts I know about Dilip Kumar, he is from a rich landlords family he joined this profession because of his passion, more than a decade whenever he was given an assignment he was totally successful in a short time, he is devoted dedicated and diehard fan of the profession, his uniqueness is he is available 24 X 7 and never he is tired moreover to touch the bottom he has a team of dozen employees as his personal and private force, comprising of highly intelligent, educated, master of martial arts with exposure to latest information technology his private force resides with him in his dream house. Sir he has very good global contacts and now he has gone into hiding to bell the cat. Commissioner concluding his speech on Dilip said I just came to know about Dilip's other side accidently, when i asked him why he refuses promotions, then he said crime detection is his passion and he is not here for earning, I am sure sir there must be much more hidden from us, in Dilip Kumar's cupboard. DGP was silent for a very long time then after sometime coming out of deep thinking said OK commissioner let us wait for 24 hours.

Chapter – 15

It was 9 am over breakfast at DREAM HOUSE Dilip Kumar enquired with Kishore, in Kamini's issue anything left and hope surveillance is over and report is complete. KISHORE replying in positive said yes report is almost over except the last piece of interrogation report to be added and with your permission I wish to interrogate the three-member gang which met Kamini at hotel resort, Dilip agreeing with Kishore's assertions said, not bad idea, but in my view best is follow them keep a vigil and when you have ample of evidence in your hand then take an appropriate step. Just calling and enquiring is meaningless. Every citizen has rights to meet any citizen and they are also at liberty to speak ill against anyone, and speaking ill about anyone is not a crime. Hope you got me Kishore accepting Dilip Kumar's advice saying trailing behind requires patience and man force moreover it is a time taking affair. Time taking affairs doesn't matter when you are confident of achieving something concrete, go ahead on this particular issue. I am with you totally. Kishore felt elevated then left the dining table bidding goodbye to Dilip Kumar he came out of Dream house....

Dilip Kumar called one of the caretaker of Dream house and advised him to call all the staff in main hall and he also went to main hall and after taking a seat sat quietly in a couple of minutes all the dream house staff members gathered in hall 3 female members and 9 male members Dilip kumar gave this group a name DIRTY DOZEN and he allotted numbers to all of them from one to twelve for example DD1 and so on till DD12, all these members were Dilip Kumar's insured private army and Dilip Kumar was aware of every members whereabouts their total particulars all the members were highly trained professionals in martial arts, IT sector, they all were also highly educated, all the DD members were well versed in many languages both read and write apart from driving skills, DD members they appear as if they are illiterate working as laborers migrated from some remote neighboring state but in reality they were Dilip Kumar's most trusted trained and transparent dedicated affective secret group. Dilip Kumar takes their responsibility literally in every way, equipping them with every necessity without their asking. It is not that they are without families they do have families and every year for 40 days all of them are given paid vacation divided in three groups 3 males and 1 female and on return of the first group the second group leaves followed by third group, in their respective houses they have declared that they are employed in gulf country. All in all Dilip Kumar was the boss of a dedicated, die hard, devotional DD group; he loved his secret staff members and vice versa. Dilip Kumar was giving instructions to all the members he was advising them to be on high alert as the crook in the present case is stupid sadist and brainless, he also instructed them to declare that he is not at home and when expected not known and also advised them to inform Kishore that I have left for some unknown destination in emergency. Leaving one line message for him, if any emergency he is just one call away. He further advised one of the member to put on his dress and cover the face with mask and wear black goggles take out Scorpio and to go out and visit Paradise, Sunshine complex, Alberts residence and Kamnis Rainbow residency, your visit to these places should present as if you are just checking them without getting down from the vehicle and after few hours roaming reach back Dream house, note if anyone is following you, if so then before reaching Dream house call DD1 and give particulars of the persons following you and then turning to DD1 he said you know what to do next DD1 in reply said Yes sir I will provide you details tomorrow if anyone is found following. OK now I will be confined in the control room for the next 24 hours. Anything specific you can call me. With this all left, Dilip Kumar entered the control room and closed the door.

Dilip was busy in making calls within state and country apart from overseas calls and sending and receiving pictures, he was instructing someone over phone to provide evidence in black and white taking time but within 24 hours. Dilip was busy in the control room. He called one of his DD members and gave an address with a picture and advised him to visit this address and make enquiry as per the instructions given on the paper. Leave right now by tomorrow before lunch I need a full report, DD member left.

Meanwhile at DREAM HOUSE At 11.30 am Dilip Kumar',s DD3 came out of dream house dressed to look like Dilip Kumar and driving Scorpio came down to Germany consulate waited there for few minutes opposite to consulate he took out his mobile and keeping it near his ears then without uttering a word kept back the mobile and left the spot from here he drove straight to Paradise and here also without getting down from the car he stood there a few yards away from Paradise in opposite direction as if he is waiting to see who will enter or exit from Paradise. From there he came down to Rainbow residency, here also wait and watch finally Scorpio entered Police headquarters here DD member entered the administrative block enquired about Kishore and after few minutes was back in Scorpio heading towards DREAM HOUSE, while on the road he noticed one black Sedan was following him after coming out of Police headquarters, he passed on the information to his counterpart with location after 25 minutes Scorpio entered DREAM HOUSE and day was called off.

After Scorpio entered DREAM HOUSE Sedan waited for a few minutes to confirm the end of Scorpio's journey, later after a few minutes Sedan zoomed away, unaware of being followed.

Chapter - 16

At sharp 10 am DGP Sharat Saxsena entered police headquarters and before entering his chamber he advised his receptionist to inform commissioner of police Karim Khan to see him at once, and entered his chamber.

After a few minutes commissioner entered DGP's chamber and after a protocol of respect took his seat both were staring at one another in silence.

DGP said the deadline of 24 hours is coming to an end in a few hours' time. Do you have any constructive information about Dilip Kumar's whereabouts. Commissioner who was literally in the dark was speechless but his confidence upon Dilip Kumar was unbreakable, gathering his guts he said Sir Dilip is expected anytime today with positive results. DGP advised the commissioner to make a call and confirm what time he is expected.

Commissioner called Dilip Kumar and from the other end Dilip advised the commissioner to take a pen paper and to note down his points to be followed. Accordingly, the commissioner took out a paper and started writing on the paper whatever Dilip was dictating. Finally, he said OK and disconnected and looking at DGP handed over the paper on which he took down Dilip's instructions.

Going through the writing on paper he said what is this, Dilip wants Paradise staff adhoc-PA Mr Gupta, an accountant and assistant to late Rajiv Dhawan, Driver Sandeep, attendant Ramlal and two security persons present on duty that day of unpleasant incident along with Raja sabs son and daughter, he also wants RIMS Dr Chandra and one security staff member present on duty that day with his in charge and one attendant Mastan Ali, he has also insisted that Ms Kamini a social worker to be summoned and lastly advocate Mohan Verma with his assistant Shrivastava. What the heck is this commissioner on what basis we can summon all these people ok somehow we have done it and if Dilip fails in proving their involvement then what will be the consequences, moreover where about Raja sab is still in dark.

Listening to DGP quietly commissioner said Sir all the listed persons are in one way or another linked to Raja sabs missing moreover we are just calling them for enquiry and nothing more than that, and above all in Raja sabs kidnapping a group must be responsible, further based upon my past experience I have never seen Dilip has ever called any unwanted unrelated person to the present issue, so I humbly request you sir let us go ahead and arrange the meeting of the listed persons accordingly. DGP nodding his head advised the commissioner to proceed.

Commissioner came down to his chamber and called his PA and gave him the list of names and advised him to call and tell all of them to be present at DGP's police headquarters by evening 6 pm today, taking the instruction PA came out and accordingly got busy in doing the task given.

At Dream house It was 3 pm Dilip Kumar came out of his control room and settled in the hall calling for a cup of hot coffee. Which was served in ten minutes, meanwhile he made a call to Kishore and advised him to reach house immediately.

Dilip was sipping coffee the same moment Kishore landed. Dilip also offered him a cup of coffee from the pot and gave him a piece of paper with an address written upon it and instructions, advising him to follow the instructions written on the paper. It is 3.30 pm now and sharp at 6.30 pm you must enter DGP's conference hall with the work done, Kishore wanted to say something but Dilip stopped him sensing he has a bundle of queries in mind, no questions please. Kishore left.

Dilip Kumar was busy at Dream House arranging the entire findings related to Raja sabs attack and missing, Alberts murder and dead body found at Sunrise complex. Dilip was feeling that he is loitering in a jungle of confusions, immersed deeply in thoughts he came out from the jungle of confusion as his mobile was ringing responding to the call, he said Sir I am on my way, call was from commissioner Karim Khan. At 4 pm Dilip Kumar left Dream house and drove casually, reached police headquarters and entered Commissioner's office seeing Dilip commissioner gave a sigh of relief and said come we have to see DGP he is more tense and because of him I am out of my mind hapless and helpless.

Commissioner and Dilip came down to DGP, he was speaking to home secretary and was assuring him that before the end of the dead line. Department will give them relief. Ending the call and looking at both officers he said the home secretary was taking my class. Anyway, what is the progress? In reply Dilip said Sir let all the listed persons gather then it will be curtain raiser meet. Dilip requested the DGP to call one group at a time and let them give a slip with names who have responded to the oral summons. Dilip Kumar came down to his chamber. Followed by commissioner Karim Khan.

DGP called PA and gave him instruction as requested by Dilip Kumar, on arrival of people summoned for talks.

It was 5.30 pm and people who were orally summoned started landing. Receiving the visitors PA to DGP advised them to give their names on a slip of paper. By this time one after another all the people as per list landed and gave their names on a slip of paper. PA through attendant sent all the slips to DGP. After few minutes commissioner and Dilip Kumar also entered DGP's chambers. DGP handed over the slips to Dilip Kumar, who after going through all the slips and putting the slips in stainless steel straight rod paper memo holder said Sir these slips will help you to prove your working, and requested DGP to call all the visitors inside. One by one all the persons were called and were seated in conference hall doors were closed. Visitors were served tea, coffee and snacks, around 6 policemen stood guarding two doors of DGP's chamber. Presence of police guarding the doors and top rank official sitting opposite to them looking straight into their eyes, it was a scary moment to the visitors. Atmosphere in the air conditioned conference hall was tense.

Welcoming the gathering Dilip said gentlemen you all are here to solve the mystery behind Raja sabs murderous attack and his kidnapping involving a couple of additional murders and to save the life of one person, to be murdered.

Chapter – 17

All the persons present were sitting motionless, DGP and Commissioner were feeling very tense, excited and experiencing uneasiness. Dilip continuing his statement said the culprit indeed is very genius but not a professional assassin nor a habitual offender. The culprit with a criminal mind taking a couple of like-minded offenders in confidence committed all these mischiefs and wrong doings. Same moment Kishore landed and coming close to Dilip said in a whispering tone work is done, Dilip advised Kishore to bring them inside and after a couple of minutes two persons on wheelchairs, in black aprons covered from top to toe, face covered with mask, and eyes covered with black goggles entered hall and were seated in a corner with four police guards around both. Dilip waving his hand and giving thumbs up sign to Kishore continuing his briefing said Mr Shrivastav visited one of the suspect Albert who was later eliminated brought him on police radar, all the visitors turned to Shrivastava and he rose from his seat and said Sir I am innocent and did not commit any wrong. Dilip with a smile said sit down

Mr. Shrivastav you are not in the red zone, continuing he said late Albert wanted to grip advocates closeness with Raja sab to acquire the land parcel near the Airport, by offering commission to which Mr Shrivatav refused and parted. Then coming to Ms. Kamini her move close to Raja sab and hiring local goons also brought her on police radar but after thorough investigation we came to know that Ms Kamini is a true social worker and she was requesting Raja sab to support her area contender in coming elections as Raja sab's one word is enough for his entire establishments staff to favor her area contestant and hiring local goons was to threaten one person who was harassing young girls from the labor community, Ms Kamini rose from her set and said Sir I am innocent, smiling Dilip Kumar said Miss you are out of danger zone. Coming to Alberts murder it was just to confuse the police as the assassin was worried that he tried to kill Raja sab but he did not kidnap him and during his trailing behind me and my deputy Kishore he learnt that as we are checking Albert the culprit thought Albert is behind Kidnapping and he hired the services of a fugitive Dara whose dead body was found in Sunrise apartments. Dara was in need of shelter and money; he was very much wanted in his home town for murder theft and molestation in his home town in neighboring state. The culprit came across when Dara was hunting for a hide out in deserted areas and by chance he came across culprit and was trapped. Dara was hired to frighten Albert to spell out if he is a kidnapper and one day Albert gave Dara a stern warning as a result the master mind offender advised Dara to kill him and in turn assured Dara to send him out of India. Dara did the job and assassin was scared if Dara is caught, he might tell police about him and he will be in police net so he liquidated Dara mercilessly.

It was pin drop silence in the conference hall. All the people present in the hall were feeling uneasy, fearing who would be the black sheep and all were looking at those two seated on wheelchairs motionless. Dilip continuing said now the killing of PA Rajiv Dhawan was very unfortunate, well I could not convey my condolences to his son who came and left after conducting last rites, anyways so I was informing you all, the death of PA Rajiv was unintentional why because that it so happened Rajiv Dhawan saw Raja sabs car was being driven by a stranger he got confused if Sandeep would have been on drivers seat he would have not bothered but strange face he took a U turn and started following the car he was confident that car has been stolen and thief is trying to go out of city, he chased the car and stopped it and started enquiring who the hell is on wheel and in this confrontation the master mind criminal also reached there and Rajiv sir recognized him and in order to conceal his identity the culprit killed him. And to confuse police he created a scene to prove that Rajiv sir was going out of the city and dumped his body near paradise, so that police should be busy with dead body, but to his utter bad luck police highway patrol came across the abandoned car and after going through papers brought the car to Paradise. The body was seen by a passerby who informed the patrol car. And as a result police were on high alert which was a first nail in the coffin of criminals.

DGP interrupting enquired Dilip who is the culprit and what was his intention behind all these wrong doings. Dilip said just a moment sir I will unmask the culprit and turning towards the visitors requested Sandeep to unmask the first masked man, Sandeep hesitatingly went near and with shaking hands removed the face mask of the masked man and with a shock moved few steps back similarly all present in the hall were also shocked because the masked man was Sandeep standing In Front of them the conference hall was dead silent everyone was mesmerized then Dilip Kumar breaking the silence said one more shock to you all the second person on wheelchair and turning to Kishore said please remove the mask, Kishore did the job and again all were enthralled and rose from their seats in shock seeing Raja sab in front of them, all were mesmerized and Raja sabs children came running and embraced their father with joy Ms Meena was literally weeping with joy. Dilip came close to her and consolingly said you are a brave heart, face things in your stride, wiping her tears she said Oh I am sorry. DGP and Commissioner were in a state of shock and enquired with Dilip what is all this to which Dilip said give me few minutes and I will reply to all your queries. First of all we will look into two Sandeep issues to know who is real then turning to Kishore said please remove the mask and when Kishore moved to Sandeep the one who was with the advocate-PA Gupta. And with unexpected swiftness Kishore pouncing upon him removed his prosthetic face mask and all present in the hall rose from their seats in utter astonishment because he was ANIL DHAWAN son of late PA to Raja sab Rajiv Dhawan. Every soul present in the hall were spellbound, police who were standing behind Raja sab took ANIL into custody, DGP asked Dilip what was his moto behind all this indecent activities, to which Dilip said money Sandeep informed him that Raja sab has written a fortune for him in his will but his father is opposing it urging upon Raja sab to change the will indeed the news was a pleasant surprise but his father opposing it made him upset because he didn't want Raja sab to change the will hence he hatched a plan with his local friend who entered Paradise with him and everything was preplanned, before the meeting he took leave from his father and called off the day then he came to transformer which was near to his house and advised his friend to switch off the main and immediately exit from Paradise the moment lights were off he rushed inside Raja sab who was seated near the door he went to Raja sab inflicted injury and came out immediately and was out of Paradise. DGP in surprise said that's all. Then turning towards the cops who apprehended ANIL said take him away and while passing near the table ANIL pushed the cops a side and leaped forward and picking the stainless-steel straight rod paper memo holder kept on the DGPs table, pierced in his heart the stab was so fatal which pierced through heart, victim died on the spot. Occurrence happened in a fraction of seconds nobody imagined it and it has happened. Body was shifted to the government hospital for autopsy.

DGP asked Dilip where was Raja sab to which Dilip said Raja sab was not kidnapped he was in in ICU after 7 hours when I went to ICU for a last check before leaving I saw ICU staff heads down on table and when I turned to Raja sab I saw movements in his body I came close him and he opened his eyes and looked at me in surprise, I signaled him to keep quite and in synopsis explained him why he is here and also requested him escape plan from RIMS so that the real culprit will come out to find out results for his action plan Raja sab cooperated and from canteen door way he escaped and I came down to control room guard was in the room with his head down on the table very conveniently I erased the Raja sabs exit footage and later from main door bidding goodbye to receptionist I came down to my car and Raja sab was in the car then I took him to my farm house rest everything is known, Commissioner asked how about real Sandeep well this is a very interesting part, Rajiv Dhawans car found on the out skirts was creating confusion in my mind hence I decided to take a look at surroundings and thereafter, as on either side of the road it is complete dense forest area so I decided to enter the forest on one side first, and after going little interior I saw a depilated condition house went closer and saw Sandeep on the chair hands and legs tied up, blind fold, mouth covered and ANIL's accomplice relaxing on the floor. I quietly returned from the spot and then back in the city I enquired about Sandeep and through his call records I learnt that Anil is in constant touch with Sandeep. Then I shifted my focus towards ANIL, I contacted overseas address and also checked with the immigrations department and the cat was out of bag. ANIL went abroad and made his presence there through one of his friend and came back to India and contacted Sandeep because he wanted to take Sandeep's place to be near to the target. A little enquiry and everything were crystal clear. Commissioner questioned Dilip then why he did not kill Sandeep, in reply Dilip said Sir he had plan of killing Sandeep throwing all the blame upon Sandeep and kill him making the murder look like suicide and police will think that Sandeep was the king pin responsible for all these misdeeds and case will be closed, and ANIL will go scot-free with his fortune.

DGP said what a show O my God it was too much for too less. Anyway, Dilip I am happy you have done a great job. Then turning to Commissioner DGP Sharat Saxsena said Karim Khan you call a press meet and declare the issue is solved and inform the media that Raja sab went on his own and came back on his own and also inform the media the tragic end of the accused.

With this thanking one and other they all parted. Raja sab thanked the police department and also thanked Dilip Kumar very profoundly. Ms Meena with father's permission requested Dilip to visit for a get-together with Kishore on this weekend at RAJA sab's farm house. After much persuasion Dilip agreed. later all dispersed.

While on the way to DREAM HOUSE Kishore enquired boss why did you call RIMS staff, Paradise staff and Advocate Mohan Verma when they were not involved. My dull head detective Calling Paradise staff was to assure the fake Sandeep that he is not a suspect.

Then calling advocate Mohan with a request to come with assistant. Calling RIMS staff was to highlight their silly lapses on account of which Raja sab could escape conveniently. Then why you did not take them to the task questioned Kishore, clarifying Dilip Kumar said this is their first mistake so I thought to pardon them by avoiding public insult but I will meet RIMS Dr. Chander and will compel him to plug the loopholes. OK, one last clarification, we were followed from Alberts residence. Oh rubbish, it was the childish act of a kingpin as he was eager to know about the Raja sab issue, so he hired drama characters to just follow us and give him the report over phone. These hired trailing couple were in trap few days ago and on interrogation they spell the beans. Kishore expressing his sympathies towards Raja sab said, Raja sab has lost a very trusted lieutenant Rajiv Dhawan, now who will take his place, mounting the portico stairs Dilip Kumar stopped and turning to Kishore said my dear friend the best choice to compensate Rajiv Dhawan's absence for Raja sab will be Ms. Kamini, why you refer Kamini's name, enquired Kishore, in reply Dilip said she is very honest devoted dedicated and daring lady out on the streets in support of destitute on her expenses and Raja sab is aware of her activities and he wanted to help her financially she politely refused stating that she will loses the charm of helping others on her own, Kishore was moved as the appreciation on Kamini was from Dilip Kumar, concluding his remarks on Kamini Dilip said I will strongly recommend Kamini's name to Raja sab when we attend party at RAJA gardens, in lieu of Rajiv Dhawan, a character never to be forgotten. And with this no more questions, we have reached DREAM HOUSE.